CW01623751

THE *compleat* LIAR

THE *compleat* LIAR

★

PENNY
VINCENZI

with illustrations by
PETE WILLMIN

CASSELL
LONDON

for PAUL
who says he believes
everything I say

CASSELL & COMPANY LIMITED
35 Red Lion Square, London WC1R 4SG
and at Sydney, Auckland, Toronto, Johannesburg,
an affiliate of
Macmillan Publishing Co., Inc.,
New York.

Copyright © Penny Vincenzi 1977
Cartoons © A.P. Willmin 1977
All rights reserved. No part of this publication
may be reproduced, stored in a retrieval system,
or transmitted, in any form or by any means,
electronic, mechanical, photocopying, recording or
otherwise, without the prior permission of
Cassell & Company Limited

First published 1977

ISBN 0 304 29885 9

Typeset by Inforum Ltd., Portsmouth
Printed and bound in Great Britain by
Lowe & Brydone Printers Ltd.,
Thetford, Norfolk

Preface

This is a book about lying. It is about when to lie and how to lie and when not to lie and how not to lie. It might make you laugh and it may make you cry.

Life is all lies. Small lies and big lies; important lies and unimportant lies. It would be a sorry world without them, and a simpler one too; life would be less charming and more chilling, less amusing and more sobering. We would talk less and think more. We would smile less and cry more.

Politicians, journalists, lawyers, publishers, advertising copywriters and fashion photographers would all be out of work. The building trade would collapse, postcards would change colour, holiday brochures would have blank pages and people would send their Christmas presents back. Few husbands would have wives and fewer wives would have husbands. And God might well be mocked.

We need to lie. We need to lie both at work and at play; in love and in marriage; in life and possibly even in death. The truth does of course have its place, but it is important to know exactly where that is. We should lie to our parents and to our children, to our lovers and our friends, otherwise we will lose the lot. But we should lie with skill and subtlety, with caution and care, with fervour and finesse. Lying is an art, a science and a skill; it needs to be studied and practised, learnt and passed from generation to generation. Some people are better at it than others — they will not need this book. Some people are better at believing lies than others — they will not need it either.

This book will help you to lie and to be lied to; it will broaden your horizons and reduce your problems. It could even increase your income. It will also make you feel rather differently about life. Things will not be quite the same ever again. For while it is a helpful book, an important book, a constructive book, it is also a disturbing book. Where once you believed you may now doubt; where once you were sure, you may now wonder. Your eyes will be opened; and you will find more in things than meets them.

Perhaps you should put it back on the shelf. Quickly.

PART I

★

1. *Why Lie?*

Because lies make life a little lovelier, that's why.

Let no one ever tell you that truth is beauty, beauty truth, that honesty is the best policy, or that if you just tell how it is everything will be perfectly all right. For it isn't, it never was, and it never will be. Truth may have its place, indeed it most definitely does, but it is a stark, unpleasing structure with no roses round the door. There are many lies told about the truth, but the worse one is that it is good for you. The truth is bad for you; it hurts you, it harrows you, it shows you things you would rather not see and tells you things you have no desire to know. You should be spared the truth wherever possible and you should spare others from it. You have a responsibility, in fact, to lie and you must start at once as you mean to go on (if you have not done so already) and not shirk or shrink.

Lying may bring you enemies, but telling the truth will bring you more. Nobody wishes to hear that their conversation is boring, that their children are obnoxious or that their house is a shining example of extremely bad taste. It does not bring a glow to the eyes and a lift to the heart to hear that our loved ones no longer turn dizzy with desire every time we walk into the room, and the things that our best friends might tell us should be chosen with great care. And don't think either that not saying anything at all is the answer; silence in these matters is not golden, it's a rather nasty dross. If you've just done your front room out in cerise silk, you want it admired and admired properly; a quick 'very nice' will not suffice. You don't want your children to be dismissed with a swift observation on how they've grown, you want their brilliance exclaimed at, their looks wondered at and their charm remarked upon. You wish to hear that the candle which Robert Redford, or Sophia

Loren, might be able to hold up to you is very weak and flickering, and as for the best friends and what they might or might not say, it is well to remember that the bonds of friendship are knotted up with lies.

If you think you never lie, just keep track of what you say for a day; you'll surprise yourself. 'How lovely to see you . . . I'll ring you back . . . we'd love to come to dinner . . . what a good idea . . . what a lovely baby . . . what a pretty dress . . . of course I remember you . . . it's in the post.'

Show me a man who says he always tells the truth, and I will almost certainly show you a liar. Some of us are worse (or maybe we're better) than some others, but we all do it, most of the time, and we do it because our happiness, our society, our very civilization, is based on the lie.

Besides, the truth-teller is not good company. His stories lack charm, and humour, and above all length. His conversation is colourless, his language literal, and his life largely without incident. He has the 'flu; he has the 'flu. He's a bit upset; he's a bit upset. His granny was a nice old lady; his granny was a nice old lady. He does not have suspected pneumonia, inflammation of the inner ear, or the highest temperature his doctor has ever seen. He is not close to suicide, in need of analysis, or under heavy sedation. His granny did not go on the streets to feed her seventeen children, or sell her hair to get them through college, or have an affair with the Prince of Wales.

How different the life of the talented liar. He walks with princes (or someone who knew one) dines with film stars (or someone who's going to be) and wins the pools (with three hundred others). He loves your company, your cooking, your friends. He finds you witty, attractive and almost irresistible. He never enjoys himself more than when he is with you, and you never enjoy yourself more than when you are with him. Look at George Washington, the most famous teller of how it was in history; who'd want to have him to dinner, or to make up a four at tennis? 'Rotten soup . . . lousy shot . . . I want to go home' — these are not phrases that fall easy on the ear.

No, the lie, and the liar, are irresistible. Honesty is not the best policy, and the truth is plain indeed. The least you can do is to adorn it a little. Add a frill here and a flounce there; a touch of colour, a dash of spice. And if you don't think you can, you're deceiving yourself. Which is as good a start as any . . .

OH PLEASE PLAY SOME MORE -
I DO SO LOVE THE VIOLIN...

2. *Why not Lie?*

Ask a truthful person why he doesn't lie, and he'll come up with a set of excuses as predictable as tomorrow. 'I couldn't . . . I'd feel so guilty . . . you always get found out . . . I was brought up not to . . . people can tell . . . it's silly . . . I'd never get away with it.' This is nonsense, for you could . . . you shouldn't . . . you wouldn't . . . you shouldn't have been . . . they can't . . . it's not . . . and you would.

It all starts in the nursery, this obsession with the truth, along with a lot of nonsense (most of it lies) about crusts making your hair curl and Father Christmas not coming to naughty children. 'Tell the Truth and Shame the Devil', you were told, and that's a lie too; never mind about the Devil, the only person you shame is yourself. 'Yes, I broke it/spilt it/lost it/forgot it . . . no I didn't make it/find it/do it/remember it.'

God is Truth, we are told in Sunday School, and maybe He is, but who's to know and if that's a lie won't we all look silly, standing at the Golden Gates waiting and waiting? And if He is Truth, then I'm not sure I want to go and join Him anyway — I plan on spending eternity in a golden glow — not being told I'm singing out of tune or that my robe needs a wash. I think we should examine the reasons for all that indoctrination a bit more closely; and it doesn't have to be all that closely actually, you can spot it a mile away. It's because it makes the lives of mothers and fathers and aunties and teachers a great deal easier.

Consider a situation; a priceless vase is found (no longer priceless or even a vase) in several hundred pieces on the kitchen floor. 'Did you do this?' says Mummy to little Fred and lifting up his huge, blue eyes the nicely-brought-up-child will say, 'Yes, Mummy I did!' End of problem; Fred can be reproached, the bits of vase put in the dustbin and Mummy can get on with whatever it was she was doing beforehand. Now supposing Fred lifts up his huge, blue eyes and says, 'No, Mummy I didn't,' then Mummy has her work cut out, unless

she's sensible enough to pretend to believe him, and get on with what she was doing anyway. First she has to question him closely; then she has to decide whether he is telling the truth; and then punish the cat, the dog, the man mending the sink or the west wind, according to what Fred's story was and what her judgment of it might be. The wilder, the more elaborate, the more difficult to disprove his excuse, the more exasperated she gets; whereas were she a thoughtful, a sensible, a worldly Mummy, she would give Fred a knowing look and send him off for the dustpan and brush!

For when Fred is grown up and he omits to send in his sales figures in time or to phone his wife and tell her he's going to be late home so his dinner's ruined, it will not stand him in very good stead if he says, 'I'm sorry, Sir, I didn't do my sales figures because I was playing darts in the pub till closing time' or 'I'm sorry, darling, I haven't phoned but I didn't actually give you a thought because I was chatting up Cynthia in Accounts.' And it might even do him a bit of good if he says he didn't do the sales figures because he'd been promised a bit of vital information on a new encouraging upturn from Stoke-on-Trent, which sadly proved to be a red herring; or that he didn't phone because the switchboard had closed down and the M.D. was plying him with drinks and telling him he had him marked down for promotion and he didn't like to interrupt and go out to a call-box.

It is short-sighted and even unkind to rear children too strictly in the tradition of truth-telling. It's a hard world, and children need all the help we can give them to get through it. It's a really rotten trick to lead them to believe that they must tell the truth, the whole truth and nothing but the truth; so help them God if they do. A bit of the truth, half of the truth, even most of the truth — that might be all right; but not all of it, not every bit of it, not nothing but it; that is all wrong. We teach our children how to read and write and do up their shoes and cross at the zebra crossing; so why not how to lie?

Now I can see this is a very new notion and it may well seem both shocking and shameful to some, but that's beside the point. It's not so very long ago since we (or at any rate our grandparents) were led to believe we had been found under gooseberry bushes or delivered by the stork, the true facts of the matter being too shocking and shameful to be told; and not so very much longer since our great-grandparents were being dreadfully shocked and shamed by the notion that we sprang not from Adam and Eve and the Garden of Eden, but from some rather lowlier creatures and a primeval swamp. What shocks and shames one group of people is matter of fact to another; and if we go ahead and pioneer new frontiers of moral education I think it's quite likely that our grandchildren and their grandchildren will think it was rather odd of us not to have helped them more in the matter of learning to lie. Because once you've left the nursery, owning up to your wickedness doesn't do a thing for you. The world, unlike Mummy, does not say, 'There, there, never mind, well done for owning up, we quite understand,' and it's bad parenthood to tell our children it will. The nasty shocks will set in early as the world says some rather different things like, 'You're fired', 'Get out' or even 'Take a hundred lines'. Then they will think of us not warmly and lovingly but bitterly and resentfully for telling such lies about telling the truth.

3. *How to Lie*

Lying improves with practice. If at first you don't succeed, lie, lie, lie again. The important thing is to begin. If you keep putting it off you'll never get anywhere. Resolve to tell at least one lie a day for a week, and then as you increase in confidence, you can step up the quantity and improve the quality. So first know your lies.

Start with the easy ones. You may be telling quite a lot already without properly realizing it. If that is so, then they are probably Negative Lies. Negative lies are the ones to cut your teeth on (you will have heard of lying through your teeth, no doubt). The negative lie consists of stopping short of the truth, of perverting it, of twisting it and turning it, but not actually launching over the hill into a positive untruth. It is just as deceptive, just as misleading as the positive lie, but it has the great advantage to the apprentice that it does not require much aplomb to carry it off. Thus:

Example 1. You are a husband. You have a new secretary. She is golden-haired, blue-eyed, long-legged. She is disturbing. You find it hard to concentrate on your marketing plans.

'What's your new secretary like?' asks your wife.

'Oh, very pretty; attractive, I suppose, if you like that kind of thing,' you say, vaguely, not lifting your eyes from the paper.

Now you have spoken truthfully. You will not be caught out if your wife subsequently comes to your office and sees your secretary. You have not said that she is one-eyed and wart-ridden and you wouldn't touch her with a barge-pole. You have said that she is very pretty and indeed if you liked that kind of thing, attractive. Quite true. But what you have implied is that you are not interested in her prettiness and that you do not find her attractive. Quite untrue. However, your wife will not give her many more thoughts, and you can continue to be disturbed by her, undistracted by spousely suspicion.

Example 2. You are a wife. It has been a glorious day and you have spent a great deal of it lazing in the garden in your bikini while your husband has had a particularly trying time locked in a meeting. You feel guilty.

'God, I feel ghastly,' says your husband. 'Another five minutes in that boardroom and I'd have murdered Carruthers. What have *you* been doing?' he goes on with a nasty, knowing look at your nicely-browned back.

'Nothing much,' you say, 'terribly boring, really, nobody came near me all day. The children went off swimming, but I stayed here in case you got back early, and I managed to do things like peeling the potatoes and shelling the peas out here so it wasn't too bad, but I'm terribly pleased to see you now!'

Also perfectly true. But you implied a day of tedium and loneliness, its nothingness consisting not of delicious idleness but of missing his company. He feels less peeved and put upon, and subsides into his gin and tonic and you can scoot upstairs and put on a slightly less revealing T shirt.

Now how foolish it would have been had you, the husband with the secretary, replied, 'My God, my new secretary's incredible, I find her most attractive', and had you, the wife with the suntan, answered, 'I've been lying out here in the sun all day doing nothing and getting brown!' By deceiving (and by deceiving without telling a single untruth) you have kept your partners happy.

So much for the negative lie. Having mastered that, you can move onto the Nearly Lie. This is useful when the negative lie alone is not enough, and a positive lie is too much. Nearly lies are perverted truth mixed with a bit of lie and a lot of implication. The result is a softly-rising soufflé of allayed suspicion. Thus:

Example 3. You are a mother. In one week's time it is your daughter's tenth birthday and she wants a cake shaped like a space rocket with her name studded on it with stars. You have to order it by Wednesday afternoon. On Thursday morning you remember that you have forgotten to do so.

'Mummy, did you order my birthday cake?' asks your daughter.

'Well,' you say, 'I didn't actually, and I know you'll be disappointed, but the thing was that those cakes are so expensive,

I discovered, that if you'd had one you couldn't have had so many friends to tea and I had to decide then and there which you'd prefer and I do hope I did right, I thought you'd rather have the friends.'

Here you have implied that not only did you remember the cake *and* you went to the shop, but you spent quite a lot of careful thought on what your little girl would most like for her birthday. You have also implied that she will have the very best that you can possibly afford for her, and that your only concern is for her to have a very happy birthday. And you can scan that example as hard as you like and you will not find an actual hard-core lie contained within it. You won't find much truth either. But as a device to deceive it is excellent. The golden rule is to sound vague. You actually feel about as vague as a cat watching a canary, but nobody else knows that.

Presentation is vital in lying, and the most difficult thing for the novice to master. If you feel bad about lying two things will happen. Your eyes will shift about and you will blush, or at least look most uncomfortable. The solution is to lie while you are doing something else, (preferably in the lied-to's interest). So you denigrate your secretary while helpfully clearing the table, or re-folding the newspaper. You knock your day in the garden while mixing your husband another drink, and explain away the cake that isn't coming while getting out paper and pencil to make a list of friends to come to the party.

Next we come to the Positive Lies. Providing you have been practising your nearly lies properly, this will not be too difficult. Jumping straight from negative to positive is much harder. Start with one where there's no one to tell on you. As you progress you will have to learn to cover your tracks, but that's really advanced level stuff.

The positive lie is quite simply a lie. It is saying something happened that didn't happen, or saying something didn't happen that did. You are safer with the former, because it's harder to check them out.

You will remember your first lie. Everybody does. So don't rush it or muff it; try to enjoy it and savour it. And don't put it off too long. Just tell it how it wasn't, and then lie back and enjoy it.

Example 4. It's your wife's birthday tomorrow. You remember after all the shops have shut. All you can rustle up is a card. This is the moment.

'Darling,' you say, 'something terrible's happened, and no I haven't forgotten your birthday, but I haven't got you a present. Not for want of trying, I've had it on order for a week, but Swanbridges have let me down, and I can't collect it till tomorrow. I'm awfully sorry — but I think you'll find it's worth waiting for.'

First principles prevail; Swanbridges are unlikely to tell on you (especially if you don't even reveal which department your mythical gift is coming from) and with luck her disappointment and/or wrath will be directed at them rather than you.

Always apologise; it's a clever touch. It makes you look virtuous and it makes you feel virtuous, and if you feel virtuous you are half-way to believing your own lie. But that's another chapter.

The more sophisticated forms of lying, or most of them anyway, do not involve saying very much that is untrue at all. They depend for effectiveness on delivery and daring, rather than invention; they are not just variations on a theme, but are refinements, elaborations, miniature works of art. They are as vintage claret to *vin ordinaire*, to be rolled round the tongue and savoured and sniffed; the danger is that one admires them so much it seems a crime to waste them. One is tempted to exclaim as one might over wine, 'An amusing little lie,' 'A full-bodied untruth' and maybe indeed one could form a lie-tellers' circle, as people have wine tasting clubs, to meet once a month and exclaim, note, exchange and appreciate one another's untruths.

THE LIE BY IMPLICATION Implied lies are told by sleight-of-tongue; they use a lot of question and exclamation marks. There is a most famous example of the implied lie told by the Master himself, Noel Coward. Visiting an appallingly bad actress after her first night, he smiled dazzlingly upon her. 'What a performance!' he said, 'What a performance!' It was, it was indeed; but he had not lied, and she was quite happy. (The repetition made it sound more convincing, apart from improving the rhythm.) Thus, 'Did you go upstairs with Brenda Fairweather at the party?' can be parried by 'Darling, as if I would,' and 'You won't forget me, will you?' by 'Angel, what do you think?'

The point about implied lies is that the lied-to can make of them whatever he or she wants; they are open to every kind of interpretation and you can always, if cornered and confronted by the truth, tell it and say you'd been doing so all along.

THE LIE BY DIVERSION These are very clever, enormous fun to tell and immensely boring to listen to, which is why they are so successful.

The following example is a true one; my friend Roger, late for a meeting, rushed in most flustered and full of apologies. 'I'm so sorry I'm late,' he said, 'but I had to take the rabbit to school, we've been looking after it for the holidays, quite a nice little thing, rather rare breed actually called a Danish Blue of all things. It comes from Denmark and its coat is a sort of bluey-grey, very pretty — they were imported at the turn of the century, well anyway, we got to school and I dropped the hutch, and the bloody thing got out, well I don't know if you've ever tried to catch a rabbit but it's extremely difficult. I was all over the playing field, finally cornered it in the goal, covered in mud, so I had to go home and change. I shall miss it actually, it's surprising how attached you can get to a rabbit, of course Danish Blues are more intelligent than most . . .' by which time the eyes of his audience were glazed with boredom, their minds totally diverted from his lateness into a desperate hope that he would stop talking, and they could get on with the meeting.

It nearly always works; if it doesn't, or if you think it won't, you could always try:

THE TRUE LIE These are very daring lies indeed, because they involve telling the truth, and nothing else; the nod and the wink with which you tell it keep you safe.

Thus: 'What did you do at lunchtime today?' asks your wife.

'Oh, I booked a room at the Dorchester and rolled about in bed with my mistress for two and a half hours,' you say. 'My goodness, this is a nice bit of beef.' The point about this one is that the truth is so outrageous that it's unlikely to be believed. The only danger with this category is misjudging what is unlikely; if your wife does think you might indeed have been rolling about with your mistress, stick to the lie. You can only tell true lies if you are absolutely sure of your ground and where the lied-to may be standing upon it.

The other variation on this one is worked by giving your lie an element of truth — the True Lie Mark II. My friend Bill had a line of mistresses laid from Camden Town to Camberley; he also had a trusting wife, some loyal friends and a subscription to a squash club. 'Playing squash tonight, darling,' he'd say as he leapt into his car every third morning or so, 'got a game with John/Mike/David.' And so he had, he would play them for at least five minutes, hurtle into the bar and have a drink, inquire after the barman's wife and charge off for some more sport with Dolores, or whoever, having done exactly what he said he was going to do, but a little more besides, which he saw fit not to mention. It was a bit hard on John, Mike and David, or maybe they played with each other while he was playing with Dolores. Anyway, he never got found out and his wife was only a bit puzzled that with all the practice he got he was always right at the bottom of the squash ladder.

THE THROWAWAY LIE This is told to impress. It is fun at parties and in any new company and it relies for success on the conversation being about something quite different. 'You must enjoy your job,' you say. 'I'd love to work in television — God is that the time? I must go soon, I've got an all-night sitting — but I don't suppose I ever will, not gregarious enough, tell me, are you in that huge place at Shepherds Bush?' This is far more impressive than saying, 'I am a Member of Parliament,' because it implies great modesty and indeed taking for granted your lofty position in life, and it also gives you an opportunity to steer away from the subject if things get sticky. 'Don't want to talk about that now,' or 'Well, every other person's an M.P. these days' will get you out of it all quite gracefully.

THE PASSIVE LIE This is told by allowing someone to believe something about you which is totally untrue. My friend, on a flight to Tangier, was accosted by an air hostess who said,

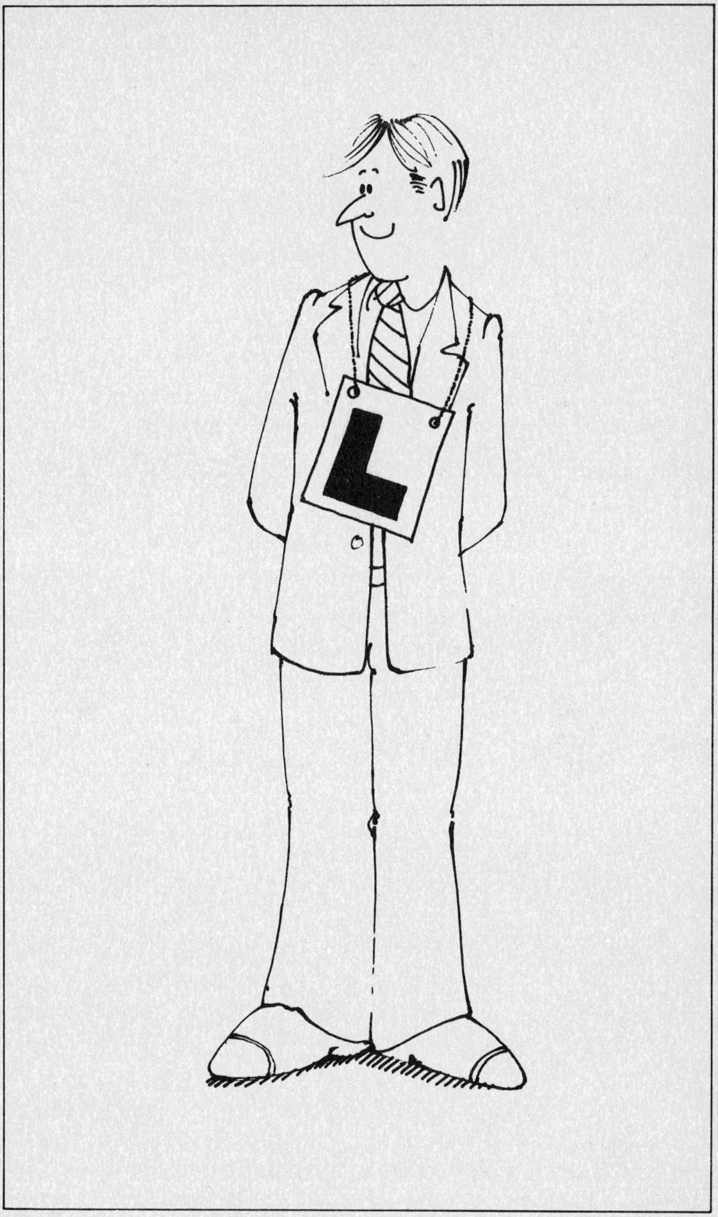

'You're a policeman, aren't you? I can always tell.' He allowed her to think so, and to assume that he was on a drug swoop or somesuch and spent the rest of the journey on the flight deck, where he was shown how to handle the controls. He finally decided he should confess. The air hostess was most indignant. 'But you said you were a policeman,' she said. 'No,' he replied. 'You said I was a policeman.'

There are times of course when it is not merely boring, but extremely rude to tell the truth; and this is when you tell—

THE SOCIAL LIE The social lie is not saying, 'I love your hair' (that is a kindly lie) but what you say when two or three are gathered together and you are required to speak. You owe it jointly to your hostess and your self-respect to tell social lies; the trick is to interest, to intrigue and to charm. 'I've heard so much about you,' you say, latching your tongue firmly into your cheek, 'and I'd simply love to hear about your accountancy practice, perhaps you could explain Schedule D to me. No, I don't play golf actually, but I do find it a most interesting game, what's your handicap? Goodness Melissa, this soup is the best I've ever tasted, I would love the recipe, yes, and where did you get the fabric for your curtains? It's so pretty, yes, I'd love some more, thank you — goodness, black pudding, my favourite. No, I don't do anything very interesting, I'm a sort of spy really, not allowed to talk about it. No, no, I'd much rather stick to Schedule D, oh, you made the wine yourselves, I'd never have guessed, it's really delicious, oh, yes *could* we see your holiday slides after dinner? Isn't Jemima divine now, so pretty, I'm sure you must be terribly proud of her. No, I wasn't asleep of course, I was just listening to the music, you always have such good sounds. No, I really must go, got to get up at six, I always do, to write my book — well it's about my work in a way, I don't really think I ought to talk about it. Yes, of course I'd love to take you home, it's not out of my way at all, now they've opened up the Westway, it won't take a minute. What a lovely evening, thank you so much, what a frightfully interesting chap old Eric is, it was so kind of you to invite me to meet him. You must come to dinner with me *very* soon and I hope you'll bring a bottle of that marvellous wine of yours . . .'

The social lie gets easier with practice; its only danger is that you get carried away with yourself. An occasional injection of brisk truth (i.e., 'I'd actually rather talk to you than see your holiday slides') will make the rest ring truer.

THE CLASSY LIE This has nothing to do with being posh. It is the lie, not the person, that is classy (although posh people are quite good at telling classy lies). The thing about classy lies is that they have a bit of vision about them; they are of some scale and substance, and very often are witty and charming as well. Saying you're late for work because you missed the bus is not a classy lie.

My friend Jenny frequently tells a classy lie about her dog. Her dog is extremely classless, and breedless too, being at least third generation mongrel. But questioned about his origins, Jenny gets a fanatical gleam in her eyes. 'He's a miniature rough-haired Italian Spaniel,' she will say, offering no further explanation until pressed. This is the clever bit; it's a throw-away line, delivered with such confidence that it seems most unreasonable to doubt what she says. Besides doggy people are incurably fascinated by new breeds, and anyway there are so many different sorts of Spaniel already, Cockers, King Charles's, American and half a dozen more, that it would not seem unlikely that Italy had thrown one up. She will then expound their history; bred with great patience and skill over a quarter of a century by an Italian Count, they are extremely rare (and of course expensive) in this country and do not yet have Kennel Club recognition, although the Italian equivalent has awarded it their gold circle only this year for the most outstanding new breed of the century, and so on. She goes on (and on) as the sun goes down and the moon comes up, her miniature rough-haired mongrel sitting patiently at her heels.

LYING FOR FUN As a sport, lying for fun should not be underrated. Lying can be a most pleasing way of passing the time, of converting a boring evening into a charming one, of becoming a riveting person rather than someone who is run-of-the-mill. Like saying your job is to dye eggs brown, or that you work for the Vatican, investigating miracles attributed to English saints. (I have friends who tell both those tales with great success, mostly because they're so extremely unchallengeable.)

Lying to shock is great fun, like announcing in trendy Liberal company that you think Enoch Powell should be the next Prime Minister, or in a staid Conservative one that you and your husband belong to a wife-swopping circle and sling in the keys every Saturday night. You have to be careful though, lest your sinlessness should find you out. My friend Angie, who lived in a sedate housing estate, put it about out of sheer boredom that her husband dealt in soft porn; she wanted merely to raise some eyebrows at a coffee morning. Three days later their next-door neighbour came round, purporting to borrow a screwdriver. Having been handed one by Angie's husband, a nice young man in the dried fruit business, he started making heavy references to screws and bangs, dug poor Angie in the ribs, and finally got out his cheque book and waved it at them. 'I'll pay quite a lot,' he said, 'quite a lot. Know what I mean?' Angie did, her husband didn't, it all got quite out of hand, and she had to confess. Her name was mud and nobody ever asked her to coffee again.

People get quite mean sometimes when lying for fun. For instance, my friend Rosie met a man at a party who happened to know some people she'd been working with. 'They all liked you except so-and-so,' he said, 'what on earth did you do to him? Quite vicious, he was.'

Poor Rosie turned pale. 'Nothing,' she said, 'nothing, I thought he was nice. What did he say?'

'Well, not much except he'd never forgive you for it. I had to change the subject, he got so worked up.'

It was no doubt fun for him, but poor Rose had a horrible evening until he told her he'd made the whole story up.

And finally the Bald Lie. Shining, simple, unadorned, it will work wonders by its very simplicity. Every once in a while forget rhetoric, poetry, embroidery and polish and just tell a good old-fashioned whopper in as few words as it can possibly take. Not often — just when you sense everything else will fail. They'll believe you.

4. *Lying from the heart*

If you don't know where to start lying, I'll tell you.

Start with your heart. That's the place all the best lies come from. Hearts are inextricably bound up with what is true and what is not. They are what you put your hand on (when you are about to tell the truth) and what you put into your eyes while you are telling it. You cross your heart and hope to die if you feel you might be about to tell a lie (best forget that one quickly, perhaps), they tend to be stout and true and, of course, they are very often fashioned of gold and together with souls are pretty well everything anyone could ever hope for.

Lying is like method acting (which is also done from the heart). You just believe in what you are saying, get inside your lie, try it for size, wriggle about in it, and adjust it where it

does not fit. You must become so immersed in it that if confronted by the truth you would be most surprised and say it wasn't there; you would not recognize it, not even if it stared you in the face. An actor does not go onto the stage and say, 'I want you to imagine that I am Hamlet,' he says, 'I am Hamlet,' he thinks Hamlet, he breathes Hamlet. He *is* Hamlet until in the end, if someone says, 'Hallo, Fred Old Chap,' he will look round over his shoulder and wonder who Fred might be.

So it is with lying. Lying is not difficult, not if it's done the right way. All that's required of you is that you should open your mouth and say things that are untrue. Doing it with panache is a bit more difficult, and that's where your heart comes in. It's no use saying one thing and thinking another; they must be one and the same. Live your lies, believe in them, and tell yourself they're true. After all, if you believe them, and you know they're lies, how can everybody else doubt it if they are led to believe it's true? You cannot lie with half your heart. It will tell on you if you do.

5. Keeping up Lies

If you care in the least little bit about keeping up with, or even leaping ahead of the Joneses, or the Cholmondeley-Smythes, then not only will you have to lie away (and away and away) like anything, but your lies will need a bit of a wash and brush up, not to mention a polish. Most self-respecting people do wish to be thought richer, cleverer and more successful than they really are, and quite right too; the others could well be labelled self-satisfied, owning up as they do quite cheerfully to modest means, sluggish wits and undistinguished careers. But for the rest of us, striving after excellence, or at least the appearance of it, the lie is our ally and our friend, our guide to higher places, our route map to the stars.

As with so much untruthfulness, it's hard to learn the rules; the three Rs of Keeping Up Lying are that the lies should be Rational, Relevant and preferably a bit Racy (they should not, on the other hand, be Rambling, Reminiscent or Repetitive). This is a lesson learnt better by example than by rote, so study the alternatives here, and then embark on a string of your own. The Keeping Up Lie falls into five sections, viz., home; work; social; cultural and financial.

HOME

Fact: *a small terrace house in an unattractive area*

Lies 1 We believe in spending our money on other things.
2 We're pioneering, of course, it's pretty rough but there are some awfully nice people moving in.
3 It was left to us by Freddie's aunt, and we get lumbered with Capital Gains Tax if we sell it too soon.

Fact: *a near-derelict workman's cottage in the country*

Lies 1 We just adore the simple life, it gives everything such meaning.
2 It's listed, of course.
3 It's so terribly Thomas Hardy, don't you think?

Fact: *an egg-box job on a modern estate*

Lies 1 Adrian's doing a sociological survey, and it helps to live in the field, so to speak.

2 It's surprisingly chic, as a matter of fact.

3 You wouldn't *believe* the things that go on here.

WORK

Fact: *you're assistant sales manager and likely to remain so*

Lies 1 Rightly or wrongly I'm just not interested in playing office politics.

2 The Old Man sees me as a threat, I'll never get anywhere until he moves on.

3 It pays the bills so I can get on with my novel.

Fact: *you've just been fired*

Lies 1 I told him where to put his job.

2 I simply don't believe in the work ethic any more, life has more to offer than that.

3 They had a purge and anyone with half a mind of their own just had to go.

Fact: *you're very badly paid*

Lies 1 Money means absolutely nothing to me, providing I get job satisfaction.

2 We're all throwing in our twopennyworth till the company gets on its feet.

3 . . . but of course my expense sheet is a blank cheque.

SOCIAL

Fact: *nobody ever asks you anywhere*

Lies 1 We don't go out much, we prefer each other's company.

2 We're both doing an external degree in Serbo-Croat and it takes all our spare time and energy.

3 We do find socializing rather trivial and unworthwhile.

Fact: *you can't afford to entertain, except on a very humble level*

Lies 1 Do come round for supper; we've produced all the food ourselves.

2 We're not doing much entertaining until the house is finished.

3 It's a breakfast party, just kippers and coffee, it's all the rage in the States.

Fact: *your origins are boringly humdrum, not a good connection in sight*

Lies 1 Of course my father was down the pits at twelve.

2 I grew up in bourgeois splendour, neo-Georgian swimming pools and treble garages, I can't bear to talk about it.

3 My parents were on the boards, I was dragged up in tawdry theatrical digs.

CULTURAL

Fact: *you haven't seen any of the new cult films under discussion at the dinner table*

Lies 1 We're into Basic Cinema — it's the folk culture of tomorrow.

2 We dislike the cinema as an art form; it's so introspective and intellectually undemanding.

3 We only go to blue films; we're thinking of making one ourselves, actually.

Fact: *your preferred reading matter is the* Daily Express *and* Reader's Digest; *those about you are into Dostoievsky and Solzenitsyn*

Lies 1 I'm too busy making money to read, I'm afraid.
2 I subscribe more to a meditative than to an intellectual philosophy.
3 I prefer writing books to reading them.

Fact: *you make an appalling cultural gaffe, revealing that you have never heard of some important artistic figure*

Lies 1 Well, I'm afraid my subject is prehistoric subterranean sculpture.
2 I'm a scientist. I only know about nuclear fission and cell rehabilitation.
3 When you've had art rammed down your throat from the age of two, you tend to react against it once you get the chance.

FINANCIAL

Fact: *you can't afford to go abroad on holiday*

Lies 1 I just have this phobia about crossing the channel.
2 We basically prefer to study our own heritage.
3 We can't bear the thought of putting Boofy into kennels.

Fact: *you can't afford school fees*

Lies 1 We simply don't approve of privilege.
2 We think private education is a very bad basis for life in the 1980s.
3 Quite honestly, the people using the state schools these days are more one's sort than the other lot, not to put too fine a point on it.

Fact: *you have to sell your car*

Lies 1 We feel bicycles are more ecologically sound.
2 I don't know about you old boy but *I'm* not getting a coronary.
3 With my back, driving's a crucifixion.

6. Male and Female Lies

Men tell one set of lies; women another. There is an area of overlap, of course, but there are certain lies which are totally sexual in origin. They do not necessarily relate to sexual matters (although inevitably many of them do) but appertain to various dilemmas, situations and predicaments which are peculiar to one or the other sex. The list here is long; you can no doubt make it longer.

MALE

I was at it long before I left school
I've never had to pay for it
I'd never be kept by a woman
You can trust me
I've had a vasectomy
My wife doesn't understand me
I got to Manchester in two hours
We seem to have run out of petrol
I'm not interested in money
I never play politics
I'm simply not ambitious
If anything happens, I'll stand by you
I was the scapegoat
If you leave the washing up, I'll do it later
I want you for your mind
All I want is friendship
I'm a bad liar
All I want is your happiness
She does 120 with a following wind

FEMALE

I wouldn't lie to you
I'll stick by you whatever happens
It only cost £5
I'm a size 10 normally
It must have shrunk
I lost five pounds in a week
I never trusted him
I'm not the jealous type
I'm not possessive
I've got a headache
I'm terribly tired
Of course I took the Pill
He's inexhaustible
My husband is earning £X,000 a year
I've never done it before
I've got the curse
I don't care about looks
I've got to wash my hair
I haven't got a thing to wear
Of course I'm interested in your work
I don't care if he hasn't got any money

MALE

You should have seen the one that got away

If I'd worked a bit harder I'd have got a First

I can't keep women off

Seven times in one night is my record

FEMALE

I'd never have anything to do with a married man

I'd never marry for money

I don't care if he fancies me or not

Of course this isn't the first time
I don't care whether the girl I marry is a virgin or not
I don't let anyone push me around
I was very fit not so long ago
I didn't fancy her in the end
Her father's eating out of my hand
I can't afford to marry you yet
Of course I want children
Of course I think he's a beautiful baby
I'm pretty fit really
I go for a run most mornings
I can still manage it every night
I can still thrash most chaps on the squash court
The place would collapse if I walked out tomorrow
The Bank Manager's a great friend of mine
I'm not easily fooled
I want my wife to have a mind of her own
I don't think women are inferior to men
My wife wouldn't mind; we have a very mature relationship
I'd have got the job if I'd been prepared to crawl
I got it on expenses
This is the first time I've ever been unfaithful to my wife
I've had a terrible day
I'd hate to be young again
I'd put up with anything for you
This is my safe period
I don't want to hear about your past
I would never try to dominate a man
All I want is a baby
I thought you loved children
I adore your mother
I don't really want a big wedding
I only want a big wedding for my mother's sake
He walked at six months
I've been cleaning this house all day
I've had it ages
I got it in a sale
I hardly ever use the phone
I hate gossip
I never gossip
The dry-cleaners was closed
I promise I won't tell a soul
I wouldn't tell anyone else
I'd never have plastic surgery
I could never deceive my husband
I'm twenty-nine
I'm prepared to do anything a man does
The phone must be out of order
I think we'd be a lot better off without men
I did tell you about it
I made it in an evening
I'd go out to work tomorrow if it wasn't for the children

7. *The Liar Cornered*

The lie, like the worm, occasionally turns. The liar is cornered, he can lie no further, deceive no more. Nothing he says can extricate him, the tangled web winds round and round him and the only thing to do is give in as gracefully as the lie allows. Here are some true stories about lies; they will make you laugh if you are a liar, and make you laugh more if you're not.

My friend Sandy worked on the till at a big casino. One night a very rich gentleman came in with a young(ish) lady, who had her hand on his arm and her eye on his wallet and the main chance. 'Okay,' he said, 'the next one's for you. If it comes up, you'll win £50,000. How old are you?'

She hesitated for a moment. 'I'm twenty-four,' she said and gave him a kiss. So he put all his chips on No. 24 and the wheel span, and the ball flew and No. 28 came up. She burst into tears and fled from the casino and was never heard of again.

If you think that's a sad story, try this one.

There was a salesman in Australia, who travelled around a great deal, putting up in boarding-houses as salesmen do, and sleeping with the landladies therein whenever he got the opportunity. He was away from home a lot, and his wife didn't know about his escapades, and we all know about what the eye doesn't see, and so on and so forth.

One night he arrived at a boarding-house, and booked in, together with an inoffensive little fellow who was also a salesman. The landlady was a widow of some charm, and she took him to bed, and he made her very happy. 'What's your name?' she had asked as they got friendly over a bottle of whisky. 'Joe Mooney,' he answered as quick as a flash, for he didn't want any trouble with his wife should she find out. Joe Mooney was the name of the other salesman who'd also booked in that night. A year later the widow died. She left a great deal of money; and she left it to one Joe Mooney, who'd given her, it said in her will, 'the most wonderful night of her life'. This story may be tragic; but it shows you what lying can do to you.

MY CAR? OF COURSE NOT OFFICER - JUST CAME OUT OF THE PUB THERE - SAW THIS LITTLE FAT BALD CHAP - SCAR DOWN HIS LEFT CHEEK - SWERVE ALL OVER THE ROAD - CAME UP THE PAVEMENT AND HIT THE TREE - DRUNK AS A COOT...
I'VE PHONED THE GARAGE BARRY - THEY'RE ON THEIR WAY...

Then there was my friend Susie. Susie does not like the truth. When in doubt she will lie. She says it makes life easier. It happened that Susie had just sent her daughter to a fee-paying school which she and her husband couldn't really afford, and it also turned out not to be a very good fee-paying school. Withdrawing the child had its problems though, but nothing Susie felt that a good lie or two wouldn't sort out. She put on a black coat, wiped off her make-up and went to see the headmistress. Susie told her that her husband was leaving her and that unfortunately she would be unable to keep the child at school. This she thought would enlist the headmistress's sympathy so that she wouldn't have to forfeit the term's fees and would be able to extract the child with the minimum embarrassment. She even remembered to say that so far nothing had been said to the child.

The headmistress clasped her by the hand and her eyes filled with tears. 'Mrs Brown,' she said, 'of course Jane must not leave. We have a charitable fund for cases just like yours. She can stay here free of charge. I will not hear another word.' Then she gave Susie a glass of sherry and the poor child is still there two years later, being badly educated, and there's nothing any of them can do about it.

And then there was a girl called Liz. Liz went to a London Comprehensive, where it was most essential for a girl's self-respect to be on the Pill by the time she was fifteen or thereabouts. At the age of fifteen Liz could stand it no longer. She went to her doctor and told him a harrowing tale of love and lust for a married man; he gave her her heart's desire and put her on the Pill. She tucked the packet ostentatiously into her satchel; honour was saved, she could hold up her head. But the boy she'd always fancied set her aside forever. 'I admired you for your principles,' he said, 'I thought you were different.' So what could she say, and who would believe her? And three years later she was still a virgin.

8. *When Not to Lie*

There are of course, times when it is highly inadvisable to lie. There are not many of them, but you should know them just the same.

Do not lie:

In a panic
In amnesia
If you're drunk
If you have a hangover
To your bank manager
In writing
In court

On tape
To your doctor
To your psychiatrist
To your lawyer
For money
In partnership
Out of spite

PART II

★

9. The Lie in Love

No one needs lies like the lover does. They are his right hand and his best friend; his guardian angel and his partner in crime. They are ingredient X in his alchemy and the ace of hearts up his sleeve; and from the moment you join the birds and the bees and the syncopating fleas, you must prevaricate and equivocate and fabricate and falsificate and dissemble and deceive until you can no longer see for the dust in your own eyes.

Without lies, love dies; it deserves more than the truth, for the truth is the harsh light of day, the cold rush of water; and neither has its place in love. So even if you have been speaking the truth and shaming the Devil all your life; if you have been cutting down apple trees and owning up to it since you were knee-high to a grasshopper, the day you fall in love is the day to change. For a truthful lover is a poor puny thing, who does not deserve so much as the scrubby humps and hillocks of a scruffy schoolboy fancy, let alone the peaks and heights of a grand passion. To scale that country takes nerve and verve and utter untruthfulness. The lover needs lies to gird up his loins — and, having girded them, to present them in their most attractive light.

Love is a two-way process and there is some two-way lying involved. You will lie and you will be lied to; and you must at least half believe all of it. The lies begin at the beginning and go on to the end when they stop.

'You are the most attractive person I think I've ever met . . . I've been plucking up courage to ask you out for weeks . . . I never thought you'd be free . . . I don't think I can possibly give you the sort of evening you must be used to . . . I wouldn't dream of letting you pay . . . I always take taxis home . . . I could listen to you talking forever.'

None of it quite true; all of it quite necessary.

Early lies give love a chance — they see that it is not stillborn — they provide the right answers. 'Yes,' when it's 'Is your steak all right?' and 'No,' when it's 'Do you mind walking home?' Keep them low profile, though, these lies — don't claim a passion for tripe if it makes you feel sick, or for moody Italian movies if they send you to sleep; that way lies lunacy, and a lifetime of Italian movies with tripe to follow.

The in-love lies are lovely. The best really, and anyway, they're nearly true. 'I think about you all the time . . . I can't sleep/eat/work . . . I never dreamt I'd meet anyone as perfect as you . . . It seems like a hundred years since last night . . . I can't think what I did until I met you . . . My life was completely meaningless before . . . what we have is an absolutely unique relationship.'

As love grows, the need for lies lessens. Sometimes, there is little point after all in lying if someone asks you if you love them. You either say that you do or that you don't and take it from there. But it's in the subtleties, the entanglements, so beloved of lovers, that the truth is torture. 'Will you always love me?' is an old favourite. The truthful answer to that one is 'I don't know'. It has to be. No one can know. 'Probably,' is a bit better and fairly truthful, but it lacks romance. Indeed all the truthful answers are hopeless. 'I really couldn't say . . . what a silly question . . . I'll tell you a bit later on.' The only one, if you love the questioner is 'Yes,' or alternatively 'Oh, yes'. And it isn't true.

Once in bed the lies come thick and fast. 'I'm usually hard to arouse . . . you've got the most beautiful body I've ever seen . . . I've never wanted anyone so much . . . it was never like this before . . . I've never had a multiple orgasm until tonight . . . you are the most imaginative lover I've ever had . . . that was the most wonderful sex I can ever remember'.

Now the thing about the bed-lies is that they just may be true, but most likely they're not. Never mind. What matters is that you're being told them. Because that means *you* matter. And you should tell them back for all you're worth. There are two bits of vital bed-truth-telling though, in answer to two vital bed questions. 'Are you a virgin?' is one and 'Are you on the Pill?' is the other. Lie at your peril.

'Do you remember?' is a minefield, because you might not, and because you might make some hideous discoveries. For instance, 'Do you remember that wonderful night in Maidenhead?' Now if you have never been to Maidenhead for anything at all — let alone a wonderful night — your answer can only depend on how much in love you are. You can say, 'Yes, darling, I do,' or 'I've never been to Maidenhead, you bastard'. But if someone is mistily reminiscing about some foolish incident, you have completely forgotten, you should smile mistily back and say of course you remember and change the subject quickly. Those kinds of conversation tend to lead on to 'But what did you do with the chopsticks after that?'

Lies of a personal nature should be told firmly, promptly and lovingly. 'Of course you're not fat . . . I love your jokes . . . you seem terribly successful to me . . . you're a marvellous driver . . . I'd love one of your watercolours . . . I adore small tits.'

The saddest lies in a love affair come at the ending of it. Learn to know them, and save yourself some pain. 'I'm terribly sorry, darling, I've got to work late again . . . I do still love you, but I feel our relationship changing . . . I think perhaps we have been living too much in our own little world — we should socialize a bit more . . . she's an old friend from my childhood . . . I don't want to hurt you . . . what we've had was so precious, let's remember it how it was . . . I love you too much . . . I don't want to possess you.' These should be countered with other, better lies, 'Oh, I'm so glad you feel that way too . . . I didn't know how to tell you before . . . I have felt a little stifled lately . . .' And best and most hurtful of all, 'I don't think we really know what love means, do you?'

10. *The Lie in Marriage*

The lie in marriage is a kindly, comforting and most necessary thing. Most marriages just couldn't take the truth; and I'm not referring to the body blows wrought by true confessions of multiple orgasms with the milkman or of blueing all next week's housekeeping on Cantering Crumpet to win the 2.30. I'm talking about ordinary life, lived out morning, noon and night in Acacia Avenue, or Rose Cottage or even Berkeley Square, by two people who may love each other very much but still tend to find each other irritating, unattractive and even unwelcome at times, and vulnerable, foolish and in need of protection at others.

It just doesn't do a marriage or the people within it any good at all to speak openly and honestly about it all the time; earthly love simply cannot survive it. (Heavenly love may manage better, but we shall have to wait and see about that.)

An entirely truthful marriage would be off like the wind, steering a course of unerring accuracy at twenty knots towards the rocks; you'd be lucky to see your first anniversary, let alone the silvers and golds. There are enough people speaking freely and frankly to you without your nearest and dearest joining in; marriage is a refuge, where you can hide even from yourself and even if you can see that your wife or husband is lying when he/she tells you how wonderful you are, you may love her or him all the more for it.

Imagine a marriage without a lie in it; how hurtful it would be, how altogether horrid from beginning to end (and the end would come swiftly).

'Not that story again, dear please, I've heard it so many times, and so has everybody else round this table . . . I didn't really expect you to get that job to be honest, but still at least you're hanging on to the one you've got . . . God, you've got boring since you've been home all day with that baby . . . Yes, actually I do find Dolores rather more attractive than I find you at the moment . . . I just can't eat this, it's awful . . . Don't

... THE REFRAIN MR JONES IS 'I DO', NOT 'COR !!' ...
1 2
1 3 7
5

start talking about your work, it literally bores me to tears . . . Since you've asked me, I don't think that dress does much for you at all . . . I knew that shelf would fall down again the minute you put it up . . . Yes, as a matter of fact, I do mind being less well-off than all our friends.' And so on and so forth.

Apart from being unkind and unattractive, that sort of thing is extremely unconstructive. The key to a happy marriage is optimism; it's seeing the best of things, and if you spend your days telling your wife she's boring and getting fat and your husband that he's neglectful and unambitious they'll get more boring and even fatter and doubly neglectful and still less ambitious, and be off with Dolores and the milkman, if they'll have them, before you can say 'love, honour and obey'.

That's where the lie in marriage begins of course, at the altar; how can you promise to love or even honour someone for the rest of your born days? It's impossible, the nearest you could get to the truth would be to say, 'I will try to,' and that would send a tremor through the Moss Bros suits. The only bit that you could truthfully say is that you'll obey for ever more, because you're dealing in certainties, but they've taken that bit out.

Getting married is something of a triumph of hope over experience anyway; it's a bit of extremely wishful thinking to believe that two people can live together happily for ever more — you're talking about castles in Spain, not semis in Surrey — but the fact of the matter is that quite often they manage it, and even enjoy it, and I suspect that the ones who enjoy it the most tell the most lies.

There's a school of thought that a husband and wife should tell each other everything, that any deceit between them damages their relationship. I reckon they should tell each other some things, and not tell each other other things, and make a few things up to tell each other along the way. Look at those open marriages, where husbands and wives sleep with everyone they fancy and are then supposed to talk about it in a frank and loving way when they meet every few days over their cornflakes. The only ones I know about are disastrous, because one partner invariably sleeps with more people than the other one and they don't talk in a frank and loving way about it, they snarl through gritted teeth if indeed they speak at all, and the marriages are so open they're a gaping, yawning chasm.

A happy marriage has lies in its bones; big lies, small lies, important lies and trifling lies; over the years an instinct will develop for when to tell what and how, but in the beginning there can be a few ground rules and guidelines. It is unwise, for instance, to lie about money or to tell the truth about infidelity. It is rash to tell the truth about the past, and pleasant to fabricate about the future. It is polite to lie about clothes you don't like and hair styles you don't admire, and rude to be truthful about a meal you don't enjoy and a present you didn't want. It is fun to tell the truth too about a happy day, and dreary not to lie about a draggy one. It is silly to lie about sex a lot but it is sensible to lie about sex a little. It is vital to lie in each other's defence and it is fatal to lie on each other's behalf. You should lie when the truth is cruel and unalterable, and be truthful when a lie is soothing but unhelpful. For as you make your bed in marriage so you must lie on it. And if you wish it to be a bed of roses, you must lie upon it a lot.

11. *The Lie in Adultery*

Adultery is of course a lie in itself. It is a betrayal, a denial, a pretence, a deceit and the only way to lend it any virtue whatsoever is to lie about it and keep lying even though trees may grow on your tongue or you are struck by lightning or any other of the well-known punishments for lying are meted out to you. (Indeed, if the tree did start to grow or you were struck by lightning, that could well be the best thing that could possibly happen to you, were you being confronted by your own infidelity by an outraged spouse, for it would provide a most splendid diversion; but alas it is unlikely, for like most of the folk-lore about lying it is entirely untrue.) It says in the Oxford Dictionary that adultery is voluntary sexual intercourse of a married person with one of the opposite sex other than his or her spouse. Presumbably if it was involuntary that would be quite all right, and that might be one of the lies you could try if all the others failed; 'I really didn't notice it was happening,' had at least the charm of originality if not the ring of truth. 'It doesn't mean anything,' on the other hand gets no marks at all for trying, and neither does 'It's purely physical,' or 'It's you I love'.

I am not attempting here to defend or even to excuse adultery, I am merely treating it as a fact of life. But it can be made less painful, less destructive, less dangerous by the use of a few accomplished lies. I do not see that anything will be gained by one partner saying to another, 'I want to tell you that I've slept with Fred/Doris and it was most enjoyable'; a great deal less will be lost if nothing is said at all, and if anything has to be said then it should imply that even if Fred or Doris had been slept with, which is by no means established and indeed a most distasteful notion, it would have been an experience of very little pleasure.

I know a liar of some distinction; her suggestion for the faithless cornered *in flagrante* is novel but worth a try, 'You should say you were extremely cold and he was trying to keep you warm.'

Now few people were born yesterday (and the few that were are seldom married) and people born earlier are unlikely to believe that particular story. But the point is that it's something to say with more charm and kindness behind it than 'We haven't finished yet' or 'John, this is Nigel,' or even 'Go away.' Anything's worth a try, because what you have to remember is that the adulteree wants to believe your lie. This is the first and greatest rule of lying in these circumstances, and the second is almost as important and is this: it is plain downright folly to Confess All when you could quite possibly get away with just a bit of the truth and a great big dollop of fabrication. Which bit is important too. Choose it with care, for it's not always obvious. One night at the sales conference might be less hurtful to hear about than a year of lascivious lunches; and by the same token a hotel bill for two makes less painful reading than a bundle of love letters. It's not the deed, it's the thought that counts, and if the thoughts are loving and poetic rather than merely lustful and prurient, then they are better kept hidden.

Back to the beginning though, and the start of the affair; and that is the time you're most tempted to tell, when it seems so harmless and charming and amusing and it is really so chilling and alarming and serious. For affairs are born of boredom, conceived in conceit, and you do wish it to be known that you are fancied, and fawned upon, and that you excite lust and lechery. But you must not talk, and you must not tell; or at any rate not the truth. This is the time to lie; remorselessly and resourcefully, by fair means and foul, by both word and implication, from Alpha to Omega, from beginning to end. Have alibis ready, not in ones and twos but in sixes and sevens. Rehearse your stories, prepare your script; enlist conspirators and be ready with reinforcements.

Keep your lies elaborate; they're harder to check on. 'We all had to go to a meeting, and then we had drinks at the Wine Bar in Soho, you know the one, and then dinner at that frightfully expensive French restaurant we went to once — God it's gone off. Then Bill insisted we went to some club or other, and I found myself sitting at a table with some sales rep. and his dreadful girlfriend, who was very drunk, and they knew a pub in Fleet Street that's open all night and we ended up there,' is better than 'I had to work late.'

Alibis likewise: 'Jane's having the children tomorrow because I want to go to Harrods, I believe they've got some sort of sale on, although if they haven't I shall probably try and get my coat somewhere else, and I'm hoping to meet Margot for lunch, although she's not sure if she can make it, and if she can't I might ring Mummy, or possibly even get my hair done, God knows it needs it. And anyway, I want to look for your birthday present,' is better than 'I'm going to town tomorrow.' Most husbands and the majority of wives will drift into boredom only half-way through; gamble on that fact and it's odds-on you'll win.

Confronted by suspicion, deny, deny it thrice and throw in some indignation for good measure. 'You must be mad' is a good phrase; so is 'I don't know how you can even think such a thing.' 'Well, I might one day but not with him/her,' is close to the wind but clever, and 'How dare you?' is excellent because you can turn the whole discussion into a thunderous row which will give you time to think. A hearty peal of laughter is a most disarming thing; and 'I'm very hurt,' and 'I thought you trusted me,' will turn the most outraged thoughts in on themselves. If you can keep your wife when all about you are losing theirs, then it's probably because you're a better liar than the rest.

It is as well to have some lies ready for emergencies; a moment's silence speaks volumes of guilt. But unless you are actually found tucked up in bed together, there are few situations so totally incriminating that they could not be explained away somehow. Confronted by the facts, lie staunchly on. People in cars can be neighbours, workmates, or your best friend's second cousin; people in restaurants can be employers, employees or your second cousin's best friend. Curious telephone calls can be faults on the line, heavy breathers or the secretary of the badminton club. Letters are difficult, but you could try, 'I knew him at college and I've always kept the letter,' or 'It's terribly embarrassing but some girl from the typing pool's got a crush on me,' and throw in 'Now would I carry it about with me if it was serious?' for good measure.

There is one masterly phrase which the adulterer should keep by him when all else fails. It explains away all but the most advanced sexual behaviour and although it carries a sting in its tail, the poison is not deadly. It is 'I'm sorry darling, but I was drunk'. Try it and see; it works, but only once.

Even when you are cornered, confronted and confounded, you should still not stoop to the truth. You owe your partner more than that. Say it was the very first time; say you were doing it because he or she had promised you a rise, or a cheap mortgage or a course of free driving lessons. Say that he (or she) was a sex therapist and you were seeking to improve your technique (and thence your marriage). Say you didn't want to; say you couldn't help it; say you can't remember how you got there. Say anything at all, so long as it's a lie. The truth may come to light; but then again it may not, and there's nothing to be gained by your flicking the switch. Adultery and those it hurts should be kept in the dark.

12. *Lying at Work*

Stop lying sometimes if you absolutely have to; the truth will out, or so they say, and if you feel it struggling inside you it might be best to give it an airing now and again. But wherever else you decide to do it, don't settle for it in the office. There's a time and place for everything, and nine to five is not the time and your office walls are not the place, for the truth.

Someone searching in offices up and down the country would find very little trace of it. And not only would he not hear the truth, he would hear an identical collection of lies. The language of the liar at work knows no frontiers; it will translate into the dialect of every company and every department, and the fugitive from the accounts department of an insurance company who has taken refuge in the sales department of a building firm will find the new tongue sounding curiously and comfortingly familiar to his ears.

'Good heavens I was just doing that,' someone will be saying to their telephone, and 'I'm just on my way out,' and 'It's on his desk for signature,' and 'My secretary didn't tell me you'd phoned.' It's actually quite unlikely, of course, that anyone should have phoned anyone to see if they were doing the Quick Crossword; or that someone who had just wandered in and hung up his coat is actually just about to rush out again, or that a letter which is written in shorthand is about to be signed, or that anyone's memory was so weak that it couldn't retain a message fed into it three times already that morning.

Once you've been out to work for a bit, you learn to translate the language, and to speak it yourself; if you're in the first week of your first job, or you're finding you're working harder than most and enjoying yourself less, you might find the glossary here helpful. Don't leave it lying around the office though; otherwise you'll have to stop lying around the office.

WORK-IN-PROGRESS LIES

I haven't quite finished reading your report . . . I haven't opened your report yet.

I agree with every word in your report . . . I don't understand your report.

I think we should call a meeting about it . . . I can't think what to do about it.

The printers have made a mess of things . . . the printers haven't had it yet.

I haven't quite checked the last set of totals . . . I haven't checked any of it yet.

The client wants it altered . . . the client hasn't seen it yet.

The client insisted . . . I like it that way.

I need to clarify the brief . . . I haven't thought about it yet.

I decided against showcards . . . I forgot about showcards.

I was just going to have that put right . . . I hadn't noticed it was wrong.

I won't bore you with the details . . . I haven't thought about it yet.

I've had to have it retyped . . . I haven't dictated it yet.

I'll get it re-checked . . . I'll get it checked.

It's almost finished . . . I'm just starting on it.

I may need an extra day . . . It's going to be late.

A most interesting idea . . . I don't quite follow you.

ABSENTEE LIES

I've got to see someone on my way back from lunch . . . I'm taking a long lunch hour.

He insisted on going out to lunch . . . I insisted on taking him out to lunch.

It's my daughter's prizegiving . . . I'm taking the day off.

I've got a bit of bother at home . . . I'm taking the day off.

I think I'll have to see a doctor . . . I'll be taking the day off soon.

I'm doing a store check tomorrow . . . I'm taking my wife shopping tomorrow.

This tooth's giving me hell . . . I won't be in tomorrow.

My great-aunt's died . . . I won't be in tomorrow.

The trains get worse every day . . . I missed the train.

The traffic was solid all the way . . . I overslept.

I think it's a great mistake to be desk bound . . . I'm sick of sitting in the office.

PRINTER
1977
...SORRY BUT YOUR JOB IS GOING TO BE LATE – THE PRINTWORKS' BURNT DOWN...
...YOU'LL HAVE TO DO BETTER THAN THAT CHUM!...
The Compleat Liar
PRINT BUYER

SECRETARIAL LIES

There was no one there when I phoned . . . I haven't phoned yet.
I keep missing him . . . I haven't phoned yet.
His secretary forgot to tell him I'd phoned . . . I haven't phoned yet.
He's out . . . he doesn't want to talk to you.
I'll see if he's in . . . I'll see if he wants to talk to you.
I did tell him you'd phoned . . . I forgot to tell him you'd phoned.
They didn't have a table . . . I forgot to book a table.
He's in a meeting . . . he's not come back from lunch (although it's four o'clock).
He's had a nine o'clock meeting . . . he's not in yet.
So sorry to keep you waiting . . . I'd forgotten you were there.

IMAGE-BUILDING LIES

My assistant's quite promising . . . my assistant does all the work.
The general opinion seems to be in favour . . . I like it.
I've done a bit of research . . . I've asked my wife.
Initial research shows people like it . . . my wife likes it.
It sold in terribly well . . . it's selling out very badly.
It was ahead of its time . . . it was a silly idea.
It's not a total success . . . it's a total failure.
Something's cropped up here . . . I don't want to have lunch with you.
I've got a panic on . . . I've got to do some work today.
I've got a crisis on my hands . . . I've made a mistake.
It wasn't my fault . . . it was entirely my fault.

BLINDING-WITH-SCIENCE LIES

The computer's messed things up . . . I've messed things up.
The computer's holding things up . . . I'm holding things up.
The computer isn't programmed to give that sort of information . . . we don't want to tell you.
You're asking a lot of our machinery . . . it won't be done in time.
The Unions won't allow it . . . we don't want to do it.

There's a hold-up at No.3 Plant . . . the production hasn't started yet.
It'll be a miracle if it gets done in time . . . we're putting on a surcharge.
It'll mean working round the clock . . . we're putting on a surcharge.
It could be done with Grontium 180, but it's cripplingly expensive . . . we're putting on a surcharge.

PERSONNEL LIES

We're enlarging the scope of your job . . . you're going to work harder for the same money.
Your personality doesn't suit this company . . . I don't like you.
There could be a board appointment . . . we can't make up our minds about you.
It's a really worthwhile job . . . you won't be paid enough.
You'll get enormous job satisfaction . . . you won't be paid enough.
The potential is tremendous . . . you're starting pretty low.
There's a salary review in the offing . . . you're going to have to wait a long time.
For the right man, the sky's the limit . . . the job's extremely difficult.

And of course . . .
Total expenses for the week £15.95 . . . total expenses for the week £5.95.

13. *God and the Lie*

An awful lot of lying goes on in the name of the Lord. There are still those who believe totally and literally in the Bible, while others see it as a pack of lies (with a few jokers thrown in) of a most colourful and often charming nature. Hard perhaps to put total faith now in the notion of a pair of solitary flower children (I wonder if they grew that kind of grass in the Garden) gambolling amongst the trees and chatting up serpents, but it is only a hundred years or so ago, after all, since Darwin was reviled and ridiculed for suggesting our roots might actually be thrust into sounder and more plausible soil. It's a pity to examine the Bible too critically though, because so much magic is lost; Moses may well have secreted a tool or two about his person when he went up Mount Sinai to receive the Law, and he may have done a quick bit of chiselling on the tablets himself before he came down again; Daniel's buddy could possibly have doped the lions; and maybe the walls of Jericho were getting wobbly well before the battle; but it would all make much less jolly reading, and is best left as it is.

Far more amazing really are the mountains of contradictions put about by the leaders and followers of sundry faiths this very day. With newspapers and television cameras making sceptics of us all, how is it that hundreds and thousands of people put their faith in the Lord being one way and in one place, when hundreds and thousands of others are following him loyally in another way and to another place?

Of course I have only looked at the religions in the most superficial sort of a way, and this is not intended as a serious treatise on theology. No doubt it's unfair to judge any religion on half an hour's acquaintance, but the fact does still seem to remain that there's quite a lot of contradiction going on.

The word of God, or rather his followers, is written many ways; which of them is the Authorised Version, only He could say. (I should think even He must be slightly confused by now as to whether His Son has, or has not, come down to join us yet,

or if it's Saturday, Sunday or Wednesday week that everybody should be worshipping Him.)

Most Christians settle for Sundays; but the Adventists, for instance, say it's Saturday. The Adventists are American in origin; Christ has come, they say, but is about to come again, and that will solve the world's ills. Believers (in the Seventh Day cause, that is) will be saved, but unbelievers will be tortured in hell, annihilated, or will remain asleep eternally, according to which Adventist division (there are several) you listen to. William Miller, an early Adventist, said the world would end in 1843, but that proved to be a lie so he changed it to 1844, and as we all know that wasn't true either.

The Jews have their Sabbath on Saturday too, of course, but don't have much else in common with the Adventists. Judaism has time on its side to lend it authenticity; it's the oldest of the one-god religions, before that gods were many and mostly local; reducing Him to One is the Jews' biggest contribution to religious philosophy and it is parent to Christianity. Jews will tell you the Messiah has not yet come, and that God has a special relationship with them, because He revealed His Law to Moses.

The Catholics also believe that they have a fairly special relationship with God. This is because Christ (who *was* the Messiah, and who *has* come), appointed St Peter as head of their Church, and the Pope is the legal successor to St Peter. The Pope is the law-giver, the Catholics will tell you, not Moses, and he is protected by God against the possibility of error (but only on matters of faith and morals).

However, the Church of England, led by that great liar, Henry VIII, says that neither the Pope nor Moses has much to do with it all. The Church is headed by the Sovereign (who is crowned by the Church). Archbishops and Bishops (who are also Lords) have quite a lot of say too, and act as a sort of State Conscience.

Most followers of the various religions will tell you that they will be going to heaven. Opinion varies as to when this might happen. Roman Catholics believe in a spell of purgatory first, doing penance for their sins, but together with Anglicans, they expect to go to heaven after death. Heaven, and getting there, is an ongoing thing, and there is room for all. Not so, say the Jehovah's Witnesses; time is running out, there is only room for a certain number and if you want to get there safely then you should hurry. By this they do not mean you should die, but that you should become a Jehovah's Witness (God's Kingdom being here on earth).

No, no, say the Baptists, what you must do is be baptised. Not as a little baby (as the Catholic Churches would have you believe) but as an adult, and by total immersion in water. The Evangelists tell you any kind of ritual is completely unimportant and no amount of good works is going to help you either; what will send you safely to the Golden Gates is faith. You will not go to heaven (the Witnesses will tell you), even if there's room, if you've had a blood transfusion, and if you are a Christian Scientist you probably won't get to heaven if you call a doctor at all. Christian Scientists say that all sickness is an illusion and if you have complete faith in the healing powers of Christ, everything will be fine. If you're a Hindu, you know that you will become another Hindu when you die, but whether it will be as a higher or lower caste will depend on how good you've been. The aim is to reach absorption in the absolute, but you'd have to be very good indeed to manage that. If you were a Muslim you wouldn't stand too much chance of reaching heaven unless you had first travelled to Mecca.

Joseph Smith, who was born in Vermont early last century, had some quite interesting things to say as founder of the Mormon religion. He unearthed some gold plates from a hillside which had certain words of the Lord written on them (shades of Moses), or so Mr Smith said, and which were translated and turned into the Book of Mormon. This book claimed, amongst other things, that the American Indians were the Lost Tribes of Israel and that Christ had appeared in America (well, it is God's own country). Mormons believe that He is coming again, and He will rule for a thousand years exactly. They also maintain that you mustn't drink tea, coffee or alcohol, but they have stopped saying you can have more than one wife. The Muslims are still saying you can have more than one wife, but they're saying it less than they were.

Buddhism is based on what Buddha himself claimed as the 'four noble truths' which he discovered when sitting under a tree (the great outdoors seems quite a good place for hearing God's hopefully truthful word). If you settled for them, rather than all the other ignoble lies, you'd give up God, who has no part in Buddha's scheme of things, and follow Buddha's eightfold path instead, which would lead you amongst other things never to take life, either human or animal, and to speak truthfully (yes, but what would you say?). You would then hopefully, and in due course, attain Nirvana and merge with universal life (which is really what the Hindus are saying) and be no more. The Hindus do have a God of sorts, whereas Buddhists settle for Buddha who never claimed to be anything more than a man, and was presumably speaking truthfully at the time.

If you are really very confused and don't know who to listen to you could become a Baha-ist. About a hundred and fifty years ago, in Iran, two gentlemen called the Bab and the Baha'u'llah decided very sensibly that God was unknowable, and that the main thing was that we should all be nice to each other. Thus Baha-ism was born, preaching religious (and also human) unity, and it is probably the fastest-growing religious movement in the world. As that is about all they say, it's not surprising. And if we all became Baha'ists I think God Himself might heave a sigh of relief.

14. *The Lie in Sickness and in Health*

Nobody can tell lies like the medics do; they lie with an enormous confidence and a casual callousness. I suspect it is not us they wish to spare pain, but themselves. It does not make their lives (which are, as we all know unsufferably busy and difficult) any easier to have to watch us weep and listen to us wail as they tell us the unpalatable truth, so they sweeten it not with the sugar of kindness, but with a sort of saccharine — a softened version of cruel lies. It is all part of their mystique; of disorientating and demoralizing us, so that we no longer know where we are, or even *who* we are. We are reduced to a pile of notes we are not supposed to read, put together in a folder with our name writ small on the front and the Consultant's writ large. not allowed to ask much, and not told anything at all.

The lies begin when you phone for an appointment with your doctor. 'He's fully booked today . . . I could only fit you in if it's really urgent . . . I'm afraid you may have to wait a bit . . . he'll see you at 5.25.' And in you go at 6.15 and tell your story of pain and anxiety, and off he goes too. '. . . I don't think there's anything much really . . . I wouldn't worry if I were you . . . it's unlikely to be anything serious . . . these attacks rarely mean anything . . . sleeplessness is not important . . . a few simple tests will put your mind at rest . . . you couldn't see a better man than Mr Harleystreet . . . all you have to do is phone for an appointment . . . this letter just tells him what I've told you . . . now these will help a lot and may even make you sleep.'

You leave clutching your letter (which of course is most unlikely to tell Mr Harleystreet that there is nothing serious in your condition and that he should not worry) to go and phone the hospital, who say you should not phone but write and you'll get an appointment straight away. Six weeks later you receive a letter which says you can come and see Mr Harleystreet at his clinic in six months' time at 11.00 a.m. You arrive at 11.00 a.m. and find a room full of people who have all been told that particular lie too, and at 12.45 p.m. you walk wearily into his room.

'Yes, yes, sit down, so sorry to have kept you waiting . . . oh yes, I remember this case . . . I'd like to examine you for a moment . . . now this won't hurt . . . nothing much to worry about . . . I can't say any more than that at the moment . . . there may be a little something there, but it's very unlikely to indicate anything . . . it wouldn't mean anything to you if I did tell you, just pop along to X-ray and we'll put your mind at rest in no time.'

So you pop along to X-ray, with a most unrestful mind, and

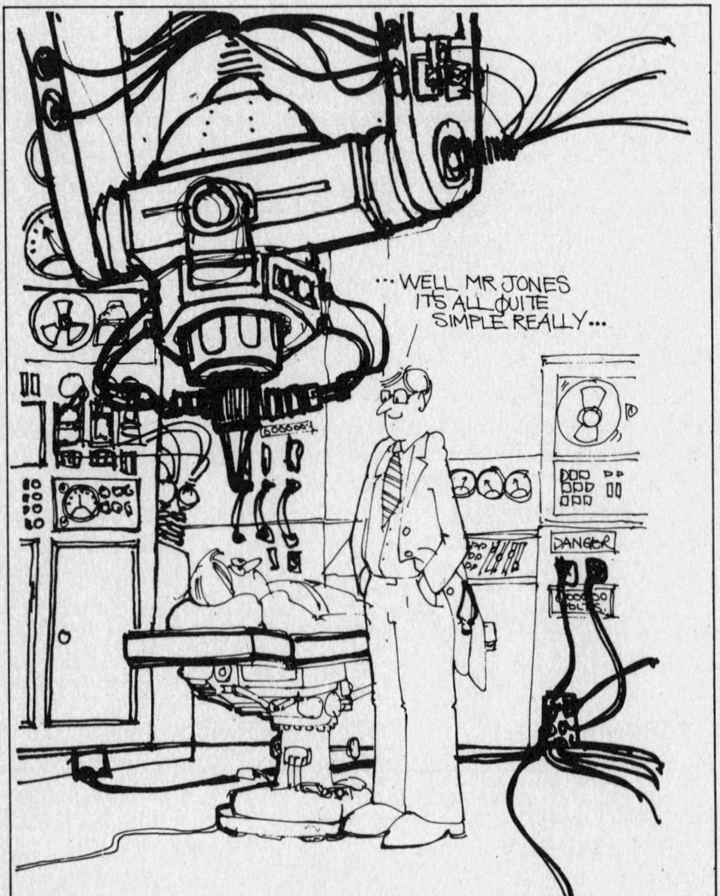

after a great deal of time you find yourself filled with unpleasant substances, possibly at both ends, with a battery of daunting equipment and an uncommunicative operator both confronting you.

The operator will not lie to you, much; neither will she tell you the truth. In fact, she is most unlikely to speak to you at all, except to tell you to keep still; although she will, when she has finished her work, instruct you to go and wait for a few minutes while she develops the plates. After an hour or so you will be able to leave.

And so back to Mr Harleystreet, some few days or weeks later; 'Oh, yes, Mr Brown, yes, well I was right you see . . . nothing to worry about really, nothing at all . . . if you come in for a day or two we'll take it out and you'll be as right as rain . . . just a very minor op., you'll be up and about in no time . . . hardly know you've been ill . . . just like a rest-cure really.'

The day of the operation dawns and finds you sitting wretchedly in your bed, cross-questioning Sister; but she has been well-trained too. 'Now Mr Brown, you know you are not supposed to ask questions . . . I couldn't tell you anything anyway . . . I think you're a fraud, you look fit as a fiddle to me . . . you'll be running round the ward tomorrow . . . I don't have your notes here . . . now, let's just take your blood pressure; yes, that's fine . . . and your pulse; yes, very good . . . I'm going to give you an injection to make you relax a bit . . . no, of course it won't hurt . . . now Mr Brown I've got more important things to do than talking to you this morning . . . you are very lucky to be under Mr Harleystreet, very lucky indeed . . . now you can stop worrying and just sign this form . . . and not long to wait now,' she says, full of '*bonne femmie*,' as if you were all going off to a holiday camp. Then, 'Oh, your turn now, you do look handsome in that gown, Mr Brown,' says a little nurse also well-trained in fatuous non-communication. 'Come on, off we go. You'll wake up soon feeling fine.'

You wake up some time later feeling terrible, sick and sore, and in quite considerable pain. 'What was it, what was the matter with me?' you ask, and 'Was it serious?' 'Now, Mr Brown,' they reply. 'You don't want to bother with things like that, you just get some rest. Now a little prick in your arm and you'll be fine tomorrow.'

And when your wretched relatives phone for information as to how you are, they'll be told you are comfortable, as well as could be expected (well, maybe that's true) doing fine, and worst of all, that you're very well (a great favourite).

And in the morning, if you are very lucky, Mr Harleystreet will be round, beaming blandly, surrounded with a different battalion of nurses and junior doctors. 'Well, well, *you're* looking well, Mr Brown . . . feeling pretty good too, I expect . . . no . . . have you out of here in no time . . . no, Mr Brown, nothing to worry about, nothing at all . . . now you can just lie back and enjoy yourself.'

Operations are bad enough but having babies is worse. Obstetricians and midwives give birth to a barrage of lies, a ghastly combination of carrot and stick, more suited to the hockey field than the delivery room. 'Morning sickness can be a bit unpleasant . . . not pains, contractions . . . you hardly feel the early ones . . . all you have to do is relax . . . and if you do your breathing right you'll enjoy the whole thing. Good, good you're doing very well . . . won't be long now . . . you may feel a bit uncomfortable now . . . why, the baby's nearly here . . . just a little push . . . just a little snip . . . you're getting on splendidly . . . come on, you can do better than that . . . there now, that wasn't so bad . . . just one more push . . .' On and on it goes until when the baby does arrive and they finally tell you it's a boy (or a girl) and it's fine, you hardly believe a word of it.

Next, the dentist! Oh, the dentist! 'You don't need an injection for that . . . just a little one . . . it won't take a minute . . . that didn't hurt did it? . . . I'll just polish it up . . . last one coming up . . . there you are you see, it was nothing really.'

But the best (or worst) medical lie I have ever heard came from a consultant, who smirked at me as I lay anxiously in my bed in an unlovely large ward along with fifteen other ladies, all about to have our ops., and said, 'My goodness, you look nice and comfy. I wish I was lying in bed, all tucked up with nothing to do but read magazines and eat grapes.' And off he walked through the dingy corridors into his big car and freedom (hospital is strangely imprisoning). It took my breath away, it knocked me out; I scarcely needed an anaesthetic!

15. *The Lie on the Couch*

There comes a point where lying ceases to be an amusing game or a social necessity, and starts to be something altogether more sinister. That is when it becomes a psychiatric condition; when terms like 'compulsive' and 'pathological' get thrown in your face, and when you begin to wonder if things haven't got out of hand. However, it is fairly unlikely that you should worry. Compulsive liars, and indeed pathological ones too, are not what they are usually thought to be. You are not a compulsive liar if you tell the gas company that there's a cheque in the post, not even if you tell them that every quarter when they threaten to cut you off; neither are you a compulsive liar if you constantly admire your friend's hideous hair, or repeatedly tell your boss you've nearly finished something when you've hardly begun it.

Compulsive liars are people who have lost touch with reality; they cannot be relied upon to tell the truth under any circumstances. They are what psychiatrists term deviant personalities; they lack a moral sense. They often suffer from a condition called *Pseudologia Fantastica,* which sounds as if I made it up, but I didn't (honestly). They make up stories which bear no relation at all to the truth, and which appear to be completely pointless. One psychiatrist listened patiently for many hours to a man describing his heroic deeds in the Second World War. The man was thirty-five. People who tell you they are Napoleon or Churchill have usually lost touch with reality.

Compulsive liars are not generally very sensible. Their lies don't seem to do much for them. I heard of one man who swore to his wife that he had paid all the bills; she found them, along with sundry solicitors' letters, in his brief-case. He wasn't lying to save himself, he simply couldn't face up to the reality of the bills and his bank balance. Compulsive lying is wishful thinking.

A psychiatrist told me that liars usually tell the truth on the couch, and truth-tellers usually tell lies. Another psychiatrist told me that compulsive liars are made, not born, by way of a loveless childhood.

You will, no doubt, hear the loveless childhood being blamed for other things too, such as a tendency to steal and to beat up old ladies (no wonder mothers are riddled with guilt). Analysis is supposed to reveal all sorts of truths that you weren't aware of, like being in love with your father or hating your mother. But I would have thought we would all be a lot better off if we carried on deceiving ourselves.

Children are compulsive liars — they will tell you their dad is a policeman, or that they know the Queen, at the drop of a hat. Mostly they grow out of it. I think it would probably be fair to say that if you are worried about being a compulsive liar you probably aren't one. If you are one, you don't know it and won't be worried about it. I don't know if the psychiatrists would agree with me, but it seems a comforting thought.

Truth drugs do work, apparently. They release every inhibition and are used quite a lot. Alcohol is quite a good truth drug. Lie detectors also work to a certain extent. They measure stress, and if a person exhibited severe signs of stress under questioning, you could probably assume that he was lying, but if he didn't exhibit any at all, you could not conversely assume that he was telling the truth.

An early form of lie detector was practised by the British Raj in India. The sahib would give his servants dry biscuits to chew before questioning them about some iniquity or other. The theory was that your mouth gets very dry if you are under stress (and lying) and the biscuits will finish it off. I found the biscuits on their own were quite enough. I once tried it before phoning through the grocery order (a fairly truthful conversation, you'd have thought) and couldn't get a single word out!

... AND JUST HOW LONG HAVE YOU THOUGHT YOU ARE ARTHUR CRUMP OF 17a BRIDGE TERRACE? ...

16. *The Lie and the Taxman*

The English tax system doth make liars of us all. It would be a stout-hearted fellow indeed who never deceived the taxman about anything, and his heart would be the only stout bit of him, for he wouldn't be able to buy too much in the way of food. The most honest people deceive the Revenue a little whenever they can (which isn't all that often) just as the most honest of people hop off the bus without paying if they reach their stop before the conductor comes downstairs again; it's common sense and a simple instinct for survival that is entirely necessary in a country which whips away a large part of what you earn without letting you even set half an eye on it. The people at the Inland Revenue deserve a great deal less than all they get and it is scarcely surprising that a great many people spend a great deal of time evolving elaborate schemes to deprive them of at least some of it.

Lying to the taxman requires a certain amount of knowledge. It's no use telling him that you've got seventeen children and nine other dependent elderly relatives unless you've got seventeen birth certificates and nine pension books to prove it. And it will do you no good at all if you say you can't pay your tax, on account of the high price of potatoes, or if you tell him that you haven't earned any money for years when you're driving about in a new B.M.W. and sending your children to Eton and Benenden.

The sad fact of the matter is that if you are a nine-to-five employee with the Prudential, let us say, there are very few lies you could tell to the taxman without him saying allo-allo-allo, what have we here, to himself. The thing is to leave the Prudential and become self-employed. Then you can tell him that you have to travel seventy-five miles to work every day; that 99 per cent of your telephone calls are business ones; that you never set foot in your car at the weekends, it's purely for business and he just might believe you and allow you to claim for your car, your travelling expenses and your telephone.

The most surprising people these days manage to be self-employed, not only the much maligned Irish labourers, but pillars of the English establishment like the milkman. What milkmen can do, should they feel so inclined, is rent their van from the Creamy Milk Co., buy the pintas outright from them and then re-sell them to their customers.

There are all sorts of amazingly tortuous things that people will do to deceive the taxman; they have their profits transferred to a country with lower taxation, by a series of dummy invoices or management charges; if they do much travelling in their jobs they will have half their salary paid in one of those countries; and they have their wives and half their children put on the board as consultants. On a lower level, if you can get paid in cash, you will find it rather tempting not to mention every penny of it; and if you ran a shop or store, you might quite easily forget that you had removed £10 a week or so from the till before you settled down and did your books.

The important thing to understand is that tax evasion is illegal, and tax avoidance is legal. Putting £5,000 in a suitcase and sending it to Switzerland is illegal. Buying a house with company money in France to use as a company conference centre, and then using it mostly for family holidays is legal. You do need to own a company though, or at least be a director of it; pilfering the money from petty cash to do it with is not really on. People do send money in suitcases to Switzerland, in case you're wondering, and even get away with it sometimes; I would have thought that with the way baggage goes astray these days you'd be lucky if it ever reached Switzerland. It would far more likely end up in Swaziland or even come straight back to Heathrow.

It is easier to deceive the taxman if you've got quite a lot of money in the first place. There is more incentive to do so anyway, because he'll be taking such a lot away from you. People go to great lengths to cheat the taxman by opening hotels for their employees to stay in cheaply, starting up subsidiary companies to run at a loss, or selling shares and buying them again, also at a loss, or looking after dependents, setting up trust funds, registering charities, and educating employee's children. If all you read was their tax returns you'd think the capitalists of England were just a bunch of benevolent old duffers, with no other thought in their heads than to see that their dependants are well looked after, their properties beautifully maintained, and much of their money given away as fast as they can make it (and before the taxman can get his 98 per cent.)

The nicest piece of tax evasion I ever heard about was effected by a barrister. He was earning much too much money in his trade, so he bought a stretch of woodland, covered in fairly infant-sized trees. Woodland takes a long time to show a profit because trees take such a long time to grow; so he just kept burying his head in his hands and telling the taxman that his trees were mopping up all his spare income. I think the trees outlived the taxman, for the barrister never had to pay the tax.

17. *The Lie in Business*

The lie in business is taken for granted. If a company's honesty were measured on a scale from nought to ten, even those sitting smugly up on the ten line would have to have slightly cloudy consciences. A business that was 100 per cent honest could not survive (or so I'm told), because it is normal business practice (or so I'm told) to bend and pretend and distort and mis-report, just a little bit more skilfully than the other fellow. And not only could the company not survive, the people within it could not survive either were they above a bit of deceiving.

Look at the simple fact of buying and selling; how much cheaper everything would be if the prices were worked out with absolute honesty, hands on hearts all over the place, and no one making half a penny more than they actually needed to. And then again how well would you fare if you confronted your fellow businessmen with the truth? 'We both know really that there's nothing special about that paint/fabric/motor oil/face-cream, and as it's a rip-off it hasn't cost us much to develop, so let's put it out at cost plus 10 per cent, and we'll still be able to feed our wives and children.' You'd be struck off the lunch list in no time, and sent to Coventry (and you wouldn't fare too well there either with all those motor cars being made; built-in obsolescence is a nice piece of dishonesty if ever I heard of it, making sure the poor beleaguered driver can't get spare parts for his dear old Banger 28½ so that he has to buy the new 32½ model at twenty-three times the price).

Businessmen lie to each other and pretend to believe each other, both between companies, and inside companies, because most of the things they market and manufacture and sell are not always entirely necessary, just occasionally not 100 per cent perfect, and now and again just a little over-priced.

Look at marketing. Marketing is the great new business science of our age. Marketing men are a new breed of smarty pants, usually dressed in over-smart pants, often a bit too fresh from university, and very often a lot too full of themselves.

They never go anywhere, not even to the loo, without their calculators, and they talk pompously about 'guestimates' and 'extrapolation' (which has nothing whatever to do with what you might think it has). Their motto, which must be engraved on their hearts, is the Right Product at the Right Place at the Right Time, and they also talk pompously about Fulfilling a Need, as if the greater good of mankind was their only concern. This is the great marketing lie. The need is usually artificially created after the product has already been thought of. Research, which is their Sacred Cow and at which no one is allowed to take a pot shot, doesn't actually discover needs; it sees an opportunity to create them. There was not really, when you think about it, an overwhelming burning necessity to create spaghetti in the shape of stars and stripes, or a cereal that sings as you pour the milk on. Children grew up well adjusted and ricketless without it and grown men did not go round beating up old ladies because they never had it. There's a need for it now all right, though; there's a frightful fuss if it's left on the shelf and little voices clamour for it whenever they're asked what they want for tea. Mankind was perfectly all right without sliced bread too, and not too badly off before gel toothpaste; but they are all an accepted part of our lives now, things we think we probably ought to try at least, just because they're there.

Marketing men lie to each other, too; they get very worked up about their targets which they have to fix once or twice a year and which are statements about how many tins of spaghetti and gel toothpaste they are going to sell. The trick is to fix your target well below where you actually think it is likely to be; then when you sell twenty tins instead of the fifteen which you said you would, your M.D. says, 'Well done, old chap,' and marks you down for promotion. You also say you will need more than you think you will in the way of money for advertising, packaging, research, development and all the rest of the unnecessary tools of your unnecessary trade, and then when you only spend £40 instead of £50, the M.D. says, 'Well done again, old chap,' and gives you a rise.

The pharmaceutical industry is also a bit dubious. It's referred to in the trade as Ethicals which sounds wonderfully upright; Unethicals more like it (only they will explain that it's

Ethicals in the sense of being on-prescription products as opposed to the ones you prescribe for yourself in the chemist). Everyone knows that the big pharmaceutical companies do wonderful things in the way of medical research, and are always stumbling upon amazing new drugs which will enable us to live to be a hundred and love every minute of it; but the fact does remain that their profits are none too sickly either.

Property men tend to be a bit deceitful too; they are more amusing and less earnest than marketing men and their lingo is more engaging; the wicked ones talk about winkling, which is getting rid of tenants by means the fouler side of fair, and the more lofty ones about planning consent and capital gains (usually their own). Property, particularly on the development side, is an area where bribery and corruption is rife. I once had a friend, who was married to a planning officer, and she said that every time he went to a meeting in the boardroom of a company, he would find something being stuffed in his pocket on the way along the corridor. Sometimes it was a roll of notes, sometimes something quite lowly like a box of cigars or a couple of tickets for Glyndebourne; it wasn't simple friendliness that put them there either. Chief Executives of local authorities suddenly find themselves able to go to the Bahamas when for years it's been Lloret de Mar; and able to lounge by their own swimming-pools instead of legging it down to the corporation one with everyone else.

Property, like the Stock Exchange, is a pack of cards game; if you have a building worth £1m and you borrow £½m on it and you want to borrow another £1m, you lie and say it's now worth £3m. If your bluff is called you're in trouble; but with skill and a bit of a following wind it won't be, and the property will actually increase in value. 'Properties,' said one property man to me, 'are not for keeping, and working and/or living in, as you'd always imagined, they are for buying and selling, and as they are bought and sold their value increases; they just make money for people.' A lot of lies are told on the basis of valuation; if someone wants a high value for capital gains purposes (so that when he sells it again his profit will appear less high) or a low one for probate (so that death duties won't be so enormous) he'll usually be able to get it. And then of course there are negotiating lies; where you're told there's already an offer of so-and-so on a property, so yours had better be better.

The Stock Exchange is not above a bit of deceiving either; stockbrokers are a jolly lot, much more fun than is popularly supposed. Their language is most charming, all about bulls and bears, insider-dealing and ramping, and a wonderful expression, 'massaging the market'. Massaging the market is a bit on the deceitful side; it's playing with share prices to your own advantage. Let us imagine that Company A is not doing too terribly well, and is short of cash; first of all you put it about that it is doing terribly well, rumours start flying around, the share prices move up (that's ramping), and when they're doing nicely you put in a bid for Company B which is cash rich — and which you get cheap because your own share prices are high.

Insider-dealing is also dishonest; in America it has to be notified to the Stock Exchange, by law, but here it's all done on the basis of a gentleman's agreement, and as gentlemen have been known to be dishonest, there is room for a bit of manoeuvre. If you work for a company which makes, let's say, fountain pens, and is doing well, and you know it's about to stop doing well because people are about to stop wanting fountain pens because ball points are about to be invented, you sell out very quickly before most people know about ball points. It might be gentlemanly to wait, but you'd probably end up in nice gentlemanly poverty if you did, and as temptations go, it's pretty fierce.

Auctioneers have on occasions been known to lie. There is something called an 'off-the-wall' price, which means that the auctioneer gambles on a room being so full that no one will notice that an opening bid or two here and there has not come from anyone at all, but has been called by an entirely mythical person standing against the wall, swiftly echoed by the auctioneer.

And what about all those directors who do nothing for a company except have their name on its writing paper and draw large fees? Not entirely honest that either, you might say, but the point is that they are chosen for their contacts and their status. They are really large, self-important sprats to catch shoals of mackerel; it does work, otherwise it wouldn't go on.

That's the whole point about business, and the lie contained within it; it's gone on a long time, ever since people started swopping a cow for three pigs, and if they could persuade the pig seller that dear old Buttercup was younger than she actually was then they might get four pigs instead.

While people are greedy, or even acquisitive, they will strive to acquire as much as they can, for as little as they can. And that inevitably involves telling a little untruth here and there, and now and again, simply to keep up with Jones & Co.

18. *The Lie in Advertising*

Advertisements lie with charm and style and skill. They are no longer quite as good at lying as they were, because sundry virtuous busybodies called the A.S.A. and the N.P.A. and the I.B.A. are all fussing about wielding blue pencils and making sure that the public is not being misled. This is a waste of their time and somebody's money, because the whole point of advertising is that the public knows that it is being misled and mostly it is quite happy to be misled. Nobody ever did believe passionately right down to the very fibre of their being that such-and-such a detergent actually gets their washing cleaner, or that a certain toothpaste would cause wedding bells to ring, or that tinned vegetables are preferable to fresh ones; their common sense would tell them otherwise. But it is quite fun to be told so, in richly evocative words and exquisitely constructed photographs, to sit back and say, 'What nonsense,' and then quite probably choose to buy the things anyway; or else settle for a brand recommended by *Which* magazine.

Advertising *is* a lie; it puts forward fallacious reasons for buying unnecessary things, but most of them are very hard to believe and it is that fact which renders it innocuous. Advertising is a seduction of a most charming, beguiling nature. 'Look how lovely I am,' it says. 'See how much better than the others. Take me, I am yours, for only £2.99 and two years to pay.' It puts the best bits forward and ignores the worst; but it does not force you to take anything. It is not rape.

All that has happened now is that the advertisements are less fun to read and less amusing to watch; because the letter of them has to be shown to be true. Oh, for the golden days of the Mileage Ingredient, the Ring of Confidence, Perfume Worth Nine Guineas an Ounce, and Dishwashing Hands as Soft as Your Face! Cosmetic advertising particularly has taken an appalling beating; once upon a time you could buy a bar of soap secure in the knowledge that nine out of ten film stars were out there in the chemists with you, or alternatively that it would make you grow a little lovelier each day; now you have to content yourself with a lot of boring mumbo-jumbo about optimum moisture balance and nature's own ingredients.

Nevertheless, unadulterated truth is still not a substance you will find a great deal of in the commercial breaks or the front and back pages of the glossies; it is bent and swayed and twisted and turned until it comes out of the advertising machine almost unrecognisable (but not quite, for the letter men of the A.S.A., the N.P.A., and the I.B.A. see to that).

Some campaigns are so patently untrue that presumably even the letter men must laugh and leave them alone. No lager in this world, nor even the next, is going to make a moustache stop drooping, or a walking stick burst into flower; and nobody, I imagine, has been round the hen coops to extract the information that nine out of ten chickens prefer Oxo.

However, it's amazing what, despite the letter men, they still get away with. There's a new car on the market called the Chrysler Alpine; it's 'The World's First Seven Days a Week Car'. Well, I bet you didn't know you couldn't drive a Mini on Sundays, or a Toyota Tuesday through to Friday. You can Take a White Horse Anywhere — not to Sung Eucharist you couldn't, it would be most out of place, either the white charger or the bottle of whisky, nor for an interview for an important job either; and as for Persil Washing Whiter, whiter than what, we might well ask. Well, whiter than before the wash went in perhaps; or whiter than blue or yellow, certainly.

Some are true, of course; Guinness *is* good for you; A Diamond *is* Forever and The Train does Take the Strain (providing it is not locked up in an engine shed while the driver and the guard have a dispute). But there are lots of substitutes for wool; not many housewives, in these hard times, are daft enough to refuse to swop one pack of washing powder for two others; and not many cats are silly enough to walk past one plate of food in favour of another.

Maybe the letter men don't read small print, but some lovely lies can be found in the small ads; 'A real family need,' cries one, extolling the joys of a ready-warmed lavatory seat. Families need lots of things, like food, love and a roof over their heads; they do not need warm lavatory seats. A gentleman offers to teach you to play the piano by post 'so that you will be

BIG
BIO!!!
biological
washing
powd
BIG
BIO
!

welcome everywhere'. I can think of a few places where you wouldn't be, even if you did do his advanced course. And I do think it's a bit rash of G-Plan to claim they have the most comfortable chair in the world.

The Country Goodness thing is a frightful lie. Fields of corn yield instant breakfast; cows in meadows drop packets of butter; misty hills give up neatly packeted peas. Nothing of the back-breaking task of harvesting, the stench of the cowshed, the heartbreak of a failed harvest. Most of the people going misty-eyed over the simple life would find it appallingly distasteful and exhaustingly complicated; but they buy the lie along with the peas and pick up a bit of folksiness with the packet of cereal.

But the lies I hate the most (and I mean this most sincerely) are the ones that imply you're a lousy mother if you don't use their lousy products. There's that poor little boy left moping outside school, all his friends long since collected, because his wretched mother doesn't use Splosh and takes too long over her floor-washing; and the pathetic little girl, big-eyed with misery, whose friend's towel is fatter than hers, because the friend's smirking mother used Soggo in the rinse-water. Those lies strike at the heart of truth; they imply that mothering has nothing to do with love, gentleness, humour or kindness; but would have us believe it is a feckless shoddy materialism to be bought for the price of a packet of soap and then thought no more about. They play on guilt, they strike at self-confidence. Those lies are dangerous; it is those the letter men should be stamping out.

19. *Lies for the Masses*

The masses get told masses of lies. It suits those who are (as they see it) our betters and in charge of us to tell us various untruths of varying degrees. These they think will keep us going quietly, being happy with our lot and generally not being too much of a nuisance to 'them'. 'They', over the centuries, have been in turn Church and State, and from time to time Revolutionaries and even perfectly well-intentioned reformers. But whether they were good, bad or indifferent, they saw fit to tell us things which can be fairly described as untrue, and to tell these lies so repeatedly that most of us believed them. They probably believed them too, but that is not the point. The time has come to re-examine all these palliatives, these stale crumbs of comfort, and see them for what they are, namely lies, untruths, falsehoods and taradiddles, or even terminological inexactitudes, whoppers, mis-statements or fibs.

There are the lies for the downtrodden (very popular these); Suffering Enobles, they are told, and Virtue Brings Its Own Rewards; Every Cloud Has a Silver Lining, the Darkest Hour Is Before Dawn (that really does keep people going) and, of course, Money Can't Buy Happiness.

The downtrodden are also told that Kind Hearts are More than Coronets, that A Fair Day's Work will be rewarded by a Fair Day's Pay, and that Right Will Prevail, so there's maybe a bit of light at the end of the tunnel. Congregations are told that God Loves Them, that as He's in His Heaven, All is Right with the World, that He Cares, that He's Everywhere and that He Helps Those Who Help Themselves.

Anyone who might seem to be loafing about a bit, staying in bed late and clearly not trying very hard is told a lot of sanctimonious lies: Be Sure Your Sins Will Find You Out, people say, and Satan Finds Work for Idle Hands to Do, and Early to Bed and Early to Rise Makes a Man Healthy, Wealthy and Wise, and of course Hard Work Never Hurt Anyone.

Over the years various well-intentioned figures have

GOD IS ON OUR SIDE...
GOD IS ON OUR SIDE

spooned out some stirring lies about All Men Being Born Equal, about Liberty, Equality and Fraternity, and some mysterious fantasies called Human Rights. Then there are the rallying patriotic lies: There'll Always Be an England, we're told, God is on Our Side, Right Will Prevail, Our Country Right or Wrong, and that to Lay Down Our Lives for Our Country is the best thing we could ever possibly hope to do.

There are lots of lies for lovers; Absence Makes the Heart Grow Fonder, Love Makes the World Go Round, and All the World Loves a Lover, and for the educated wooer, *Amor Omnia Vincit* — Love Conquers All — which is rubbish in any language.

Women are spooned out a lot of sexist lies; that they are the weaker sex, that their place is in the home, that their name is frailtv, that their price if they are virtuous is above rubies (which would seem to imply they weren't often) and that The Hand that Rocks the Cradle Rules the World.

There are a few soppy lies to cheer people up a bit; Nature is Wonderful and Knows Best, There's No Place Like Home, (and East, West, Home is Best). Children are told that Schooldays are the Happiest Days of Your Life, which they do seem to know is a lie, and the lower classes are told that the Battle of Waterloo was Won on the Playing Fields of Eton (which the upper classes still believe). There are even some lies about truth. How many times have you been told that Honesty is the Best Policy or that Truth Will Out? And up to now I daresay you believed it.

20. The Lie and the Public

The public is very seldom told the truth. It is lied to from morning through till night by shopkeepers, civil servants and hairdressers. All manner and kinds of tradesmen and builders are liars *par excellence*. Forewarned is a bit forearmed; recognize the lies and you're half-way to outwitting them. This is only a sample selection, but you'll find it a help.

AT THE DRY CLEANERS

You must have it re-textured.
Really it needs the *de luxe* treatment.
It'll be back on Thursday morning.
That sort of fabric requires special care, it's 10 per cent extra.
The buttons were very loose when it came in.
Of course it's not lost.
We did take every possible care with it.
Really it's a fault in the manufacture.
You couldn't expect anything else.

TALKING TO THE BUILDERS

The factory's clean out of copper piping.
My cement-mixer's broken.
I've got three men off sick.
The van's in dock.
There's an overtime ban.
I can only get brickies to work Sundays.
That's not a straightforward job, I'd have to charge you extra.
There's a hold up on wood.

IN THE TAXI

This is the only way to Buckingham Palace.
Piccadilly's worse than this.
Trade's terrible these days.
I've got nothing against the private motorist.
What with the rise in diesel and the cost of my cab, I hardly make anything these days.

AT THE RESTAURANT

The strawberries were flown over from Switzerland this morning.

It's all gone, but I will ask the chef to make one specially for you.

It's made with fresh asparagus, Spring lamb, and double cream, marinated in wine for three days and simmered in brandy, served with a little . . .

It's so nice to see you again.

For you it's a pleasure.

AT THE BEAUTY COUNTER

This is made from extract of seaweed and rose thorns crushed in pomegranate juice, to revitalize tired cells.

This may seem expensive, but it goes through 163 processes before coming up to our standards.

You do need the night cream as well.

It's very reasonable really — it will last you a long, long time.

This really will make your nails strong.

It's the new autumn colour from New York.

Now with that lovely eyeshadow, you can't possibly wear your old lipstick and blusher.

I always use this myself.

AT THE TAILOR

Your shoulders are a little round, that's why it hangs like that.

Trousers are narrower this year.

That looks very smart.

A waistcoat is essential with a suit like that.

A small adjustment, and those trousers will hang perfectly.

IN THE SHOE SHOP

You'll need this special spray.

It only looks like that because it's real leather/a new acrylic fabric.

They'll lose their shape in no time without these trees.

They're not really coming apart, it's just the welding.

You must realize you can't wear shoes like that in the rain.

They're fully waterproof.

We've never had a complaint like this before.

You do walk rather heavily, madam.

IN THE BOUTIQUE

That looks really lovely on you.
It's the latest line from Paris.
You really shouldn't wear skirts any longer than that.
If you just moved the buttons over it would be perfect.
We have very easy credit terms.
We've sold dozens.
It washes beautifully.
It won't shrink.
You won't get it cheaper anywhere.

AT THE HAIRDRESSER

I really do think you'd look better with a very, very short cut.
That colour looks a little old-fashioned now, you should have a change.
I'll be with you in a moment.
Mr Gavin is our very best cutter.
Our champagne and strawberry shampoo and a double cream treatment will help those nasty split ends.

AT THE SUPERMARKET

Fresh in Today!
New!
3p Off!
A real bargain!
Buy now and save!
Price increase imminent!

AT THE ESTATE AGENT

Four good-sized bedrooms.
Large garden.
In reasonable repair.
There are a lot of people after it.
They won't consider a lower offer.

AT THE GARAGE

You can leave it like that, of course it's up to you, but you'll never get it past the M.O.T.
It might be differentials, or it might be your fly-wheel, I can't tell without stripping it down.

It'll be ready at five o'clock.
I'll take it off your hands for fifty quid.
One careful lady owner.
It's not the parts, it's the labour that costs the money.
It's not the labour, it's the parts which are expensive, as it's a foreign car, you see.
It's easier to get foreign parts than English ones these days; now if you had a V.W. I could turn it round in no time.
What rust?
You won't have any more trouble with her now.

21. *The Lie in Politics*

Everyone knows that politicians lie all the time. They lie six times before breakfast, seventeen times after lunch and every single thing they ever say to anybody concerning the running of the country is totally untrue. That's the folk-lore, anyway; like most folk-lore it has a question mark or two hung over its head. Politicians do lie (politics is after all a business, much like any other, and indeed business has quite a lot to do with it, rather too much, some people would say) but they probably don't lie quite as often as we all think they do.

It is not so much that they are intrinsically noble, truthful creatures, who would infinitely prefer death to dishonour, battling their way through in a relentless pursuit of the truth; it is more that it's not nearly so easy for them to lie as you might think. There is a most effective lie detector in politics called The Opposition. There simply is no other profession where everything you say is chronicled and where over half your colleagues spend just about half their time waiting to catch you out in any kind of inconsistency at all.

Consequently, although a lot that is said in politics is not entirely true, most of what is said is certainly not wholly a lie. Politics is not actually a business of black and white, it is nearly all extremely grey, and the men who work in the business are extremely grey also. And even when they tell apparent whoppers, such as in their election manifestos, they are not quite so wantonly and wickedly misleading as they might seem. The point about manifestos is that they are simply advertisements and advertisements put forward the good news more plainly than the bad. But unlike advertisers, politicians are required to be seen to be delivering, and when they don't, as they usually don't, there is a great deal of uproar.

However, when they work out their manifestos, they are acting in surprisingly good faith; they do think that they will be able to deliver. People after all don't like being lied to, and if they are clearly going to discover that they have been lied to, they will obviously be extremely cross and upset. The promises

do of course continue to be made and continue to be broken, as night follows day, but this is not because politicians are hardened, dyed-in-the-wool liars. Some of them may be very hard, and the dyes may be very hectic, and of course they want to get into Parliament so naturally they will tell us what we all want to hear. But there is also another more scientific and reasonable reason, which is that until a party is in power, it has no access to various and vital information from the Civil Service because the information is highly confidential. Therefore, when a would-be Prime Minister promises that he will reduce prices at a stroke, it is probably little more than a highly informed guess. It is nevertheless a guess made usually in fairly good faith, and an intention of what he thinks he can do. Then he gets elected and the senior civil servants start saying, 'But, Minister, you can't,' and 'Minister, it doesn't,' and the prices do not get reduced, not by any number of strokes, and we all wonder why we even half believed it in the first place.

Often we don't believe, of course, and the whole thing backfires; so great is public cynicism in these matters that very often promises of panacea can lose elections. It is widely believed that Gaitskell lost the 1959 election because he promised sweeping tax reductions and people just didn't believe him, and George Brown once prophesied very low mortgages with the same result. Quite right too, you might say, the public are not fools, but sometimes it goes right round the other way. Lord Woolton said in 1951 that he and his boys in blue rosettes were going to abolish meat rationing and bring back good red meat; Harold Macmillan likewise put his hand on his stoutish heart and said he would build 300,000 houses in a year. There were cries of 'Lies' ringing round the House (and the country too, I daresay) but the fact was that the ration books went and the houses rose.

However, we need not waste too much time climbing into our sackcloth and hunting round for an ash or two and asking our leaders' forgiveness for all the harsh thoughts we might have been having about them; for you have to add to all that the observation that politicians might learn, along with the rest of us to regard their own propaganda with a little more suspicion. They tell the truth for expedient reasons and they bend it wherever they can, which takes the edge off any pious hope. In spite of all that I have just said, lies do get told and falsehoods do get put about, and the second half of this chapter will make more exciting reading than the first.

There are the standard quite dreary political lies, like Chancellors of the Exchequer denying that they are going to devalue until the very last minute to protect the pound, and Prime Ministers denying that they are going to call an election until they can't go on denying it any longer, and the moment seems nicely ripe. Both of them are lying and know that they are lying (and most of the people around them know they are lying too) but they go on doing it because it is politically necessary.

But there is also the occasional, more exciting political lie, such as Suez (when the Tory Government denied hotly that they were in collaboration with Israel, when as we now know they most certainly were), or when Mr Profumo denied equally hotly that he was having anything at all to do with Miss Keeler, when as we all now know he most certainly was. The Profumo lie was particularly interesting, because although it was a lie about peccadilloes rather than politics, it could fairly be said to have brought down the Government. It didn't bring the Government down because Profumo said something that wasn't true, however, but because the Cabinet, and more importantly the Prime Minister, believed him and so were seen to be, in the fullness of time, a collection of complacent and gullible fools. Though we may not be disturbed by Profumo's private life we would be disturbed indeed to hear a Premier mumbling away about how he couldn't know everything that was going on, and that is why Macmillan's army toppled, and Home appeared in shining armour to save the day and lost it to Harold Wilson twelve months or so later.

Harold is, of course, a master of the sleight-of-tongue, but it is very hard to catch him out. He can be observed in his deviousness quite often, for instance, when he changed his mind about issues (we all remember the Common Market and statutory wage and price controls) but he would no doubt defend them on the grounds of political ethics. There is a genuine dilemma here; if you lead (or follow) a party which would seem to you to have the mix right, then it is a great temptation to swallow the one ingredient which you feel is wrong along with the rest. You put your party before your principles; you lie for the common good. And that is a defensible thing to do.

A lot of political lying goes on across the sea (and especially it would seem, the Atlantic). Mr Nixon puts our lot to shame, and look at Mrs Rabin caught out fiddling her expenses, and poor old Madame Mao, lying away to everyone, including the Chairman; were any of his Thoughts dark ones about her, I wonder?

Lloyd George doesn't seem to have been especially truthful;

in a debate in the House on the shortage of munitions in the First World War, he insisted that there was no shortage, no shortage at all, when he knew quite well there was an appalling shortage. He should also get absolutely top marks for a brilliant piece of deviousness when he insisted on reviving an ancient ceremony and presenting the Prince of Wales to the people at Caernarvon in 1911. There was no ancient ceremony; he had made it all up but it went down a treat with the Welsh, although not poor Edward, who looked a bit silly dressed in white satin.

Politicians lie by image and implication quite a lot too. Gladstone was supposed to have spent his leisure hours cutting down trees (it's hard to see what good that could do him in the eyes of the public, although I suppose you need to be quite strong and manly to fell an oak) but he actually hardly ever went near one, except when there was an official visitor to his home when he would rush out and grab an axe and start showing off. Baldwin had a nice healthy, homely image of being a gentleman farmer, when in fact he scarcely knew an egg from a chicken, and certainly not which came first; and of course left-wing politicians have to be frightfully careful that they are not seen in public smoking Churchillian cigars and knocking back double brandies or generally enjoying all the other trappings of wealth and luxury, which some of them undoubtedly do in private. But my favourite political lie is not concerned with politics, but politicians; it is gossip, but it is true gossip. It concerns an Honourable Member who had a most charming and beautiful wife, and a rather dishonourable Whip who fancied her. Every now and again, the Whip would say that it was quite imperative that the Honourable Member was in the House for a vote on this or that, and that night he would scuttle off to the Member's house, his wife and his bed and they would be undisturbed for hours and hours. But one night, the vote came early — the Member returned home unexpectedly and there they were — and division bells rang like anything. However, the Whip married the Lady and they lived happily ever after; which only goes to prove that politics, like fairy stories, can sometimes have happy endings. And fairy stories are a pack of lies, too.

22. *The Lie in History*

History is riddled with lies. People set great store by historical fact, but the fact is quite often fiction. Time Will Tell, we are told, and time does indeed and it also reveals some frightful whoppers as it goes along. What numerous people believed for many years, and not only believed but fought for and died for, is quite often entirely and indisputably untrue.

Of course, people in history lied as they went along, like every other sort of people; kings lied to ministers, queens lied to kings, generals lied to their armies and Popes lied to anyone who'd listen. But they were mundane, commonplace lies, like Henry V telling his army they were going to be fine, and Richard III saying the Princes had nothing to do with him but had died of a nasty chill, and Henry IV being amazed that Richard II had been murdered, and even going so far as to go on a pilgrimage to do penance.

It would take an encyclopaedia to recount them all; the best ones, my favourites, are *real* lies, huge, imaginative, breathtaking whoppers of such grandeur and vision that they deceived, and deservedly so, on a vast scale. They did this because they followed, and indeed illustrated similar principles to those laid down on these pages; it is therefore not only interesting but also instructive to study them.

They are the Popish Plot, the South Sea Bubble and Piltdown Man. The Popish Plot lie, which was told in 1678, was about prejudice and propaganda; a lie the masses were ready and waiting to be told as its authors knew full well. They studied their market, swooped in and made a kill. Their timing was perfect, their delivery skilful and their attention to detail magnificent. They lied from the heart (see page 19). The fact that their hearts were black and dastardly is neither here nor there. As liars they deserve a place in the Hall of Fame.

The authors of the Popish Plot were two unattractive people called Titus Oates and Israel Tonge, Oates being the ringleader. He wanted to discover a real Jesuit plot, and when he couldn't find one he just invented one. It was totally and utterly untrue and it was believed implicitly. The whole thing takes one's breath away. The important thing to realize, which Oates realized very well, was that the good (and the bad) citizens of England were worried about popery. Charles II was on the throne; his brother was actually a Catholic; and everyone was worried to death that the throne of England might once again be sat upon by a Roman Catholic. So when Oates announced that he had discovered a conspiracy to dispose of the King and replace him with his brother, the Duke of York, no one was in the least surprised. They said that they had suspected as much, and even that they had known it all along. They actually only had to tell one person. The stone, having then been dropped in the rather murky pond of English political life, spread in ever-widening ripples with enormous speed.

Oates and Tonge told the Earl of Danby, who was a courtier of a greyer shade of white. He then told the Privy Council and the Privy Council told the King. Oates and Tonge were cross-examined for two days but nobody managed to trip them up. It was a lie of great class, of course (see page 17). There was nothing second-rate about it. It made interesting hearing. It was not a plot hatched by small-scale revolutionaries — the common man seemed to have very little to do with it. Its very incredibility made it credible.

Among those involved were the Pope, the King of France and the Archbishop of Dublin. It was also supported by five Catholic peers and there were, said Oates and Tonge, thousands of Catholic fanatics who would at a given signal rise up, murder the whole of Protestant London and burn it to the ground. The King, they said, warming to their tale, would be waylaid by Irish ruffians, stabbed by Jesuits and shot by silver bullets, and if that wasn't enough, poisoned by the Queen's physician.

The King laughed derisively at such nonsense as he thought it; everyone else gasped and tended to believe it. They might have stopped at gasping had not fate, a fair old liar herself, stepped in to support Oates's claims. A large correspondence was discovered, between Edward Coleman, the Duchess of York's secretary, and some prominent Catholics abroad. They said some fairly harmless, if indiscreet things, about the growing power of the Duke of York, but the fact that they were written in code turned them into dynamite. After all, if you put the weather forecast into ciphers it would sound sinister. The other thing that happened was that the magistrate, one Edmund Godfrey, to whom Oates and Tonge had made their testimony, was found murdered. These two events were taken as proof of the plot. The country was plunged into hysteria. Catholics' houses were ransacked, people persecuted, and there was a witchhunt for priests; mobs marched, banners were waved and popish books were burnt.

The lying Oates became a national hero. He was installed in Whitehall and given a state pension. A truthful Catholic silversmith who merely remarked that Jesuits were honest men, was installed in Newgate prison and accused of Godfrey's murder. Several people were executed, many were thrown into the Tower and dozens more were piled into prisons. Thirty thousand Catholics fled from London, and Catholic peers were expelled from Parliament. And all this because two men had told a barefaced, brazen, entirely unsubstantiated lie. If they had told the truth no one would have believed them.

The South Sea Bubble was a Nearly lie (see page 10), told on a very grand and impressive scale, by some very grand and impressive men. It was also a lie of optimism. It relied much on the mood of the hour, which was one of daring and adventure and entrepreneurial excitement. But its roots were in greed and exploitation and it cost people their livelihood, and some even their lives. It was blown (and burst) in 1720. There were three great financial corporations in the City at that time; the Bank of England, the East India Company and the South Sea Company, which was founded by a gentleman called Robert Harley in 1710. Its directors were the wealthiest men in England; their power was immense.

In 1720, the country was in a state of financial turmoil. Everyone was building and trading away and, in spite of having spent a great deal of money on sundry wars, there was still plenty of money around. The only thing about the money was that lots of it was borrowed, mortgaged and lent; the overdraft had already been invented. Moreover, the Government had a big one (about £30 million), and the Directors of the South Sea Company hit on a plan to rescue it, which involved some fairly high-level lying. And because of its imaginativeness and grandeur, and because it had a lot of the truth about it (see page 13) the lie worked for quite a long time.

What the Directors did was buy up the National Debt. They sold people shares in the company, which they claimed had a brilliant trading record in the South Seas. Indeed, they went on, it had a monopoly and therefore it could not fail. With the money they raised they took over a large part (about £7 million) of the country's debt; of course they did not mention that at all, which was a lie of omission.

The nearly lie concerned trading potential. There was some, but it really was extremely small. The whole scheme wasn't spectacularly profitable anyway, and was also dependent on special privileges being granted by Spain (which she wasn't really granting in actual fact). All in all it was a wonderful, spectacular hoax and people rushed to the Company with their money. In this way the lie, which was cumulative, grew and grew and the value of the stock was soon multiplied. The Government, of course, was hopelessly involved, particularly the Chancellor of the Exchequer (the plan was even approved in the House of Commons).

All manner of politicians and courtiers, and even royal mistresses, had been paid bribes in the form of fictitious holdings in the stock, in order to perpetuate the myth. In due course the company offered loans on stock held which sent the rate soaring even higher. (This particular manoeuvre, along with a few others, was masterminded by Sir John Blunt, which is a good reassuring name for a liar to have.) It was a sort of midsummer madness, and the heatwave held right through till August, when Sir John's last attempt to force up the price of the stock failed, and the bubble burst. The truth was out — everyone realized they had shares in nothing much at all and it was all very tragic; but one must still admit it was a masterly and most perfectly polished lie.

But my favourite lie, the one which takes my breath away, is the Piltdown Man affair. This was an intellectual lie — a concept of such wicked joyfulness and such original vision that one can only stand and wonder at it. It was unabashed Lying for Fun (see page 17). Moreover, it did nobody any harm at all; a few people had slightly pink faces and a few more did a bit of extra work, but in the overall scheme of things those are not wildly important considerations. Somebody (nobody seems to know quite who, and how he or she remained silent all these

years I really can't imagine) discovered a hitherto unknown forebear of ours.

The remains of a human skull, with an ape-like jaw, and some worked flints and other such archaeological delights were dug up at Piltdown in Sussex in 1912. It was supposed to have belonged to the early Pleistocene period, and the point about it was that it seemed to throw some doubt on our evolutionary sequence. With this new discovery the facts didn't quite fit; everyone was greatly puzzled, but the fun lay in it not being just the likes of you and me who were puzzled (we could have been more easily forgiven for being so) but scholars of great repute in their field were also baffled. The controversy raged for many years, on a most lofty scientific level; until in 1926 the graves were found to be not half as old as the experts had thought. This caused a few wise heads to shake and in 1953, new techniques such as X-rays and chemical tests, revealed that the teeth had been tampered with (Pleistocene dentists were very rare!) and the bone fragments had been deliberately stained.

The whole affair proved to be an enormous hoax, a most marvellously and intricately created lie. The skull had belonged to a modern man and the jawbone to a modern ape. But for forty years, everyone believed in the true existence of Piltdown Man. I think that means the Piltdown Man story wins the game. It stuck pins in pomposity and made nonsense of knowledge. If that doesn't make you believe in lies, nothing will!

Are You a Five-Star Liar?

A test paper for would-be liars. The purpose of this quiz is not to assess whether you're a liar or not, but whether you're a good one. Answer all the questions truthfully and see how accomplished at lying you are (and how much you have learnt from this book).

1 *It's your mother's birthday, and she phones to thank you for some flowers which you did not send. Do you*
Say 'I'm glad you liked them.'
b) Ask her which florist delivered them, and then phone them for more details.
c) Send some more anonymous flowers, in case the original sender phones up.

2 *Your next-door neighbour spends all Sunday putting seedlings in his garden; your dog spends most of Monday digging them up. Do you*
a) Say an old gipsy woman came round selling flowers and her dog got into the garden.
b) Ship Fido swiftly over to your mother and then in between gasps of sympathy, tell your neighbour casually that the dog's at the vet for two days having his ears seen to.
c) Say you saw two small boys in the garden, now you come to think of it, and offer to accompany your neighbour to the police station to give a description.

3 *You have accepted an invitation to go to a very boring bridge evening with some people down the road. At twenty-four hour's notice you're asked to go to a First Night with a party afterwards. Do you*
a) Develop a raging sore throat and high temperature.
b) Say your father is quite seriously ill and you feel you should go and be with your mother.
c) Say your firm has suddenly got the chance of winning a big new contract and your boss has hauled you over to his place to work right through the weekend.

4 *Sitting peacefully at a dinner party, an acquaintance suddenly asks, 'Who was that lovely lady I saw you having lunch with yesterday?' Do you say*

a) It couldn't possibly have been me, I was locked in the board-room all day.

b) Oh, that's Blenkinsop's new assistant. He'd promised her lunch and then dragged me along too, and what's worse, he rushed off after the soup saying that he had to go to an urgent meeting.

c) You're not going to believe this, but she was a long-lost second cousin twice-removed of my Boss; he practically forced me to take her out, and even tried to make me employ her, but no thanks; lovely maybe, but extremely boring.

5 *You have omitted to do some really vital piece of work for a meeting which is due to start in an hour's time. Do you*

a) Ask to have the meeting postponed till the afternoon so that you can deal with an urgent inquiry you've just had by telex from New York.

b) Create a diversion by asking if anyone has noticed how extraordinary the figures from Scotland are.

c) Say that your secretary took your stuff home to type and the idiotic girl managed to leave it there, but you've sent her to get it and she'll be back in a couple of hours.

6 *You've told your husband a new dress only cost £15; your best friend arrives in an identical one and says, 'Isn't £35 a lot for something made of cotton?' Do you say*

a) I had mine made by that marvellous lady round the corner. She copied it from a magazine and it only cost £15.

b) I got mine for £15 from the thrift shop.

c) Mine only cost £15, it's got a faulty thread through it.

7 *You've asked for the day off to take your sick mother to hospital; settled comfortably in your seat at the Seven-a-Side match you see your boss looking at you with beady eyes from three rows up. Do you*

a) Vanish at once, so that he thinks he's had an hallucination.

b) Say your mother was so grateful for your help she gave you the two tickets as a token of her gratitude and it seemed churlish not to use them.

c) Introduce your companion as Mr Wetherspoon from Smithers & Co., one of your biggest customers.

8 *Your wife finds a strange lipstick in the glove compartment of your car. Do you say*

a) The babysitter must have left it there when I dropped her home the other night.

b) Isn't it yours? It was lying on the front path yesterday.

c) It belonged to that awful woman we dropped off from that party three weeks ago, don't you remember?

HOW DID YOU DO?

Mostly (a)s. You are a spur of the moment liar; you fib first and think afterwards. You are a bit unimaginative too, and tend to overlook details. Your lies usually need follow-up action.

Mostly (b)s. You are a good, original and talented liar, but you are a little foolhardy, and you'll often need to cover your tracks with further lies.

Mostly (c)s. You are a brilliant, careful and creative liar; you cater for every contingency. Your only fault is to get carried away by your own rhetoric.